The Dancing Floor

Also by Michael M. Mc Namara

The Vision of Thady Quinlan

The Dancing Floor

by

Michael M. Mc Namara

F
m
c.3

Crown Publishers, Inc.   New York

Inquiries should be addressed to Crown Publishers, Inc., One
Park Avenue, New York, N.Y. 10016

Printed in the United States of America

Published simultaneously in Canada by General Publishing
Company Limited

Designed by Rhea Braunstein

The lines from "Byzantium" by William Butler Yeats appearing in the
epigraph are reprinted with permission of Macmillan Publishing Co., Inc.,
from Collected Poems by William Butler Yeats. Copyright 1933 by Macmillan Publishing Co., Inc., renewed 1961 by Bertha Georgie Yeats.

The excerpt from The Hamlet by William Faulkner, Random House, 1940,
is reprinted with the permission of Random House, Inc.

Library of Congress Cataloging in Publication Data

Mc Namara, Michael M   1940-
    The dancing floor.

    I. Title.
PZ4.M1704Dan [PS3563.A3234]   813'.5'4   77-20654
ISBN 0-517-53249-2

To Eilis
Who has filled
My life
With light

Marbles of the dancing floor

Break bitter furies of complexity,

Those images that yet

Fresh images beget,

That dolphin-torn, that gong-tormented sea.

from "Byzantium" by William Butler Yeats

Chapter 1

The four men in gray plastic raincoats and black berets huddled together, protecting their cigarettes from the wetness. Below them lay the main Dublin Road, a sheet of rain and mist on this late April morning. Occasionally, the monotony was broken by the streak of an early newspaper lorry or commercial van as it ploughed its way from Limerick and towards the brightening sky to the east. But the men's attention was not directed at the road. Instead, their eyes never left the boreen that spliced itself with the thoroughfare and then angled west, mounting a green rise and sinking downwards to the lake.

The tallest of the men looked at his watch. "He's late," he said. "The bloody bastard must have had an extra cut of cake with his morning tea."

"And maybe a spot of marmalade."

"Or a poached egg to give him strength with his daily calendar," young Daly said as he fidgeted with the red neckerchief about his throat.

They were becoming restless, though no one of them would have been the first to admit it. The rain didn't help. Adventure was always marred by it on this island, the tall man thought.

His reverie was distracted by the elbow in his side. "Here he comes," Liam Daly said. "You're up, Brendie."

At first, Brendan Donnelly had difficulty in following his fast moving target. As he grasped the Armalite firmly in his hands, he prayed that the official Mercedes below him would slow down—but not *too* much. He needed some of its speed for his purposes. He shifted his weight. He had it perfectly now. Just right.

At least half a minute passed before the Mercedes reached the designated spot. Donnelly carefully investigated his target through the telescopic sights, moving the cross hairs first to the driver, an awkward looking gawk in a peaked cap. It would certainly be something to see that one with a load of lead in his arse, Donnelly thought. He rotated the sights to the rear. There was his man. Cool as a cucumber. Patrick D. Mulcahy, Minister for Justice. The gunman dawdled on the key figure. Look at the cut of him, he said to himself. Elegantly dressed. Half-glasses down on his nose like a bloody professor. A cigar in his mouth. The morning paper on his lap.

Donnelly drew a deep breath. The Mercedes disappeared for the slightest moment and then suddenly was in full view again. He could see the spray of water from the tires gradually lose force. The car was slowing. Now was the time. The others were giving him their full attention. He squeezed the trigger with an even and deliberate pressure. He felt the kick of the weapon before the wind brought the crack of it back against his face.

His aim had been accurate. The Mercedes left the road and was spinning wildly in the middle of a swampy field. It would take a lorry and a crane to pull it out.

The other men congratulated him. "Right on the dot," one said. "I watched it through the field glasses. Straight into the left front tire."

"Up to his balls in mud and pig shit. Won't he be a sight in tonight's paper! His Loyalist friends up North won't be too proud of him after this."

"A lot of justice he'll be dishing out today. They'll run him out of chambers for sheer stink!"

A fifth man started the Landrover, which lay hidden behind a cluster of blackthorns. He waved for them to hurry. They'd have to be going if they were to put in the call to the *Limerick Leader*. Their contact would be waiting with his camera and notebook. They would have Mulcahy's picture in the afternoon edition, at any cost.

Chapter 2

Colum Donnelly lay awake in the old bed. It was that time of the very early morning when the first hints of day filtered through the fog and drizzle. The result was an eerie pallid light, enough for only the rooks and starlings to take heart and screech out their tongues in excitement. If he could just muster their small enthusiasm!

He hated Fridays, or rather he favored them only after the school bell struck four and the hooligans in his charge had left him alone in the chalky classroom. Before that moment, Fridays were a madhouse, and he dreaded to face them. But he had to be up. He had a reputation for punctuality. He couldn't ruin that and he only a month or so on the job. It had been downright decent of the Christian Brothers to offer him the temporary position in the first place, especially after his shameful return from their novitiate at Carrick-on-Shannon. And Brother Roland had confided that it was almost a dead cert that he'd be hired for the new year.

He shivered as he eased out onto the cold floor. St. Senan's had been a palace. Wooden floors. Central heating. Rugs. And now back to this. Cement. Sooty fireplaces. Tarpaulin. Why had he ever given the Brothers the notion that he lacked the necessary religious fervor? Hadn't he been the top of his class? Hadn't he attended every service? Hadn't he made the highest marks in teaching practice? It was the stories that had done it, the few short stories he had submitted to *The Irish Press*, the small bundles of words that Diarmuid Fagan, the editor, had praised so highly. He cursed them now and tried to regain his old humility. It was impossible. He felt the very suggestion of the fictions give brightness to his day.

When he entered the kitchen, his mother turned from the electric cooker. "Oh, you're up," she said. "I thought that maybe you caught a cold and were taking the day off."

"No, Mama," he said. "I can't be taking days off. I'm lucky to have the job, you know that."

"Isn't it tonight that you're seeing the Sullivan girl again? Mind you, it might not be the proper thing to do if you've caught . . . "

"I'm as healthy as a horse." He knew it! Jesus Christ! Once a priest, always a priest. And in Ireland, once a Brother, always a Brother. Wrong! But who would be the one to tell a woman of sixty-five that she was wrong in what she had believed all her life, that in a real sense she was a heretic in bequeathing to a layman the attributes of priesthood?

To change the subject, he said, "Where's Brendie?"

His mother did not answer, but instead she hurriedly moved the saucepans on the cooker, drowning his words. At last he caught it. He should have guessed. It wasn't the Brother thing alone. He looked suddenly at her face and noticed the redness below the eyes. "He didn't come home?" he said.

"Who?"

"Who my eye, Mama! Why didn't you call me when he wasn't in by midnight? I know where he hangs out. I could have gone up there."

"You could have done nothing. He's older than you are. He knows his own mind. It's me. I worry too much."

"A lot of worrying he does for anyone."

"Stop it this minute. Eat your breakfast, or it'll turn to grease on the plate. Hurry up now. I have to wake Josie before she's late again. One of these days, they're going to close the Boot Factory gate in her face."

It was useless arguing. He sat down at the table and began his meal of sausages and rashers and black pudding. Patriotism! Johnson might have put it all in a nutshell. And yet he could not call his brother a scoundrel. Brendan of the wild ways. Brendan of the thousand birds' eggs. Brendan the "moocher" from school. Brendan of the swims across the treacherous Shannon. Brendan the talked about, the praised, the cursed . . . He was a riddle, at the least.

Josie came into the kitchen. She ran her hand through her brother's hair. "How's my brother the teacher and lover?" she said.

He mumbled an obscenity under his breath, and reaching up he trapped her hand. He drew it to his mouth and kissed it gently.

"Oh, my," she said, "but aren't we romantic today! I'm glad I amn't that little Sullivan girl. I wouldn't want to be in the dark with a randy monk like you. Lord knows what you'd be up to."

He looked across at his mother. She was stooped over the grate. She had not heard.

Chapter 3

Brendan Donnelly stepped out of the heavy rain and into the darkness of Laffey's Public House on Roche's Street. He shook his brown topcoat and gray peaked cap before putting them on the rack inside the doorway. For a moment he blinked in the poor light, then he gradually regained his sight. The place was empty except for one customer seated in the far corner. It was his man. He walked slowly in that direction.

The face that looked up at him from the sawdust and empty Guinness barrels had the pinch of death about it. The eyes were set like huge dobbers in a shroud of gray flesh. "Brendan," the wide mouth said. "Brendan Donnelly, sit down."

Donnelly obeyed his superior, Taig Riordan, Chief of Southern Command, Provisional I.R.A. It was not often that such meetings were arranged. The boyos usually received their orders from intermediaries. This was a rare honor.

"What will you have?" Riordan asked.

"Just a pint, please," Donnelly said, touching his face nervously.

"Won't you have a small Power's with that? It'll warm you. You deserve it after today's bit of work."

"Ah, no. A pint will do."

"All right, if you say so."

Riordan waved to the bartender who seemed to have appeared from nowhere. He made a sign for two pints, then he turned to his guest. "Yes," he said. "A fine bit of work. I can't wait to see your man's face on tonight's paper. They tell me that Slattery got a powerful shot of him."

"He did? Good."

Riordan looked at him out of the darkness. "Where did you get to be such a marvelous aim?" he asked.

"In the L.D.F. I spent two years with them."

"Very nice. You let the buggers train you, and now you're using the knowledge against them. Very nice, Brendan."

Donnelly absorbed the praise. He had prayed for a moment like this since he'd joined the movement. And it had taken until today for it to come. He hadn't known of the meeting up to an hour before, when he dropped off the Armalites in Adare and sat by the fire, petting the armory dog, Blazes. Bunty Foran, the ordnance officer, had simply said, "A call just came in a bit ago. Riordan wants to have a look at you. Be at Laffey's a few minutes after twelve."

When the bartender had left their tray, the old man spoke in a low tone. "Tell me," he said, "how long have you been with us?"

"A year. It was after my father . . ."

"Yes."

"I was a bit . . ."

"Since that time, you have been on two other jobs—all expertly performed, I might add."

"Thank you."

"All what we call skirmish work."

The sudden change startled Donnelly. What did Riordan have up his sleeve? One minute it was praise. Was it now to be taken as a sneer?

"As I was saying," Riordan went on, "you have been involved in skirmish work and have done a powerful job of it. There will be more, too, as you may guess. We need to do all the embarrassing we can before the elections. We must make those bastards in the Dail look like proper eejits in the eyes of the common people. It is skirmish work that sets them on their heels. We must turn the mob against them. We must make them look no better than their Constabulary friends up North. Then we'll have them by the short and curlies. Long live the true Republic!"

"Its health," Donnelly said as he raised his glass. But in his mind he felt a certain uneasiness, a combination of the subtle slight and the coloration of Riordan's estimation of the people. Certainly the Dail had to be cleared of self-serving politicians, but to regard those of the land as senseless . . .

Riordan's voice came at him like a knife. "You're fed up with these little blowups, aren't you?"

"Oh, no . . ."

"We know. We've been watching you."

"But . . ."

"It's only natural that it should become routine after a bit. But the danger is that you might become careless, Brendan."

"That wouldn't happen, you know that."

The Chief spoke slowly. "Yes, I suppose that it wouldn't be intentional. But to tell you the truth, I am a bit concerned. How many men did you have with you this morning?"

"Four. Daly, Ryan, Keough, and Duff."

The older man paused before asking, "Were that many necessary?"

"No. But they're in the movement up to their ears just like the rest of us. I saw no harm in giving them the experience."

"Yes. But, Brendan, you can't be sure of anyone until you have something over his head. That Daly lad has never been on a caper before. We have little hold on him. He's just a schoolboy."

"Well, he's christened now, by God."

Riordan waved again to the bartender. He reached out and touched Donnelly's arm. "Don't get me wrong, Brendan," he said. "I didn't come here to reprimand you. I came down to congratulate you, really, and to tell you that the small jobs will soon be at an end. We'll be moving you up to more dangerous work. No more shooting out tires for you. So you see my point about secrecy?"

"Yes, I do."

The bartender arrived. He placed the second pair of foaming glasses on the table and left with the empties. When he had gone Riordan said, "There's no trouble explaining your absences at home, is there?"

"No. No."

"Your brother, he doesn't suspect?"

"No. The misfortune is not the same since he came back from the monastery. The life's gone out of him. He just lives in the books and school. Mahony's bookshop is his second home, I swear. I blame them Brothers. They took something away from him."

"No girls?"

"An occasional one. A student or two from the college at Plassey. There's a little one, Sullivan's her name. He's taken her out more than once."

"I've read and admired his work. He's a smart man."

"You have?" Brendan's voice was high with excitement.

"Yes, indeed. Because I'm a soldier does not mean that I am above the influence of the Muse, as one might say."

"He had a few stories in *The Press*. They were that good?"

"They were powerful. You didn't read them?"

"No. I'm ashamed to say it. Himself and myself don't have much in common anymore. Times were when you couldn't blow us apart with a ton of dynamite."

"Tsk. Tsk. Shame. It's too bad we couldn't have the two of you within the organization. What a team you'd make—your precision and his voice. He has no interest?"

"Not really. He calls us a bunch of jackeens and black-guards. His idols are men like Mao Tse-Tung and Rommel. He says that they had real style and power. We're just running around like dogs following their tails."

"That's what he says?"

"Yes. But he thinks quite a bit of yourself and others."

"McDavitt?"

"Yes."

"Well," he said and laughed, "he can't be all wrong then. It takes all kinds. But give him my regards. Tell him that I asked for him."

"Oh, God, I will."

"Try to convert him."

"To be sure."

"And now I must be off," Riordan said. "Keep the heart up. You'll be hearing from me."

"Right." Brendan extended his hand. He felt the parch-mentlike flesh of the Chief's fingers. But the brittleness was not to be mistaken for frailty. This man had spent two years behind the wire at Long Kesh.

When Riordan reached the doorway, he was obliged to sidle past a young man who was seemingly taking shelter from the rain. "Excuse me," he said. But the man paid no attention. He just stared into the grayness outside.

Back in the corner, Brendan was beckoning to the bar-tender. "Bring me another Guinness," he said. "And bring a small Paddy's, too, as you're at it."

Chapter 4

A t a bar in the Sandmall, a man sat nursing his glass of Harp. Several others on the stools were discussing the incident. "It was a foreigner," one said. "Sure there's none of our own that could hit a tin can."

"A Yank or a Dutchman."

"Naw. It was one of Paisley's lads. They don't want Mulcahy's peace neither. They'd like to tear the country apart like our own fellows."

Liam Daly made circles with the butt of his glass. He took another drink of the Harp. He turned slowly on the stool. "Ah, fuck the lot of you," he shouted. "You'd be surprised if you knew that the man with the Armalite has friends and relatives in this parish, wouldn't you?"

With that, he rose off the stool and left by the side door. The house fell into silence. Feet stroked the damp sawdust. Not a glass clinked.

A man in a tweed cap was the first to move. He walked in the direction of the jakes. An Armalite, the lad had said. The afternoon paper hadn't mentioned a word about the type of weapon used. It might have been just a wild guess on Daly's part. But still it was worth passing on. The Guards would offer a fiver, at least. And there was always the other side, so terribly shaky about leaks.

Chapter 5

A s Colum Donnelly left the Christian Brothers' yard, he felt the cold wind in his face. The rain was changing to sleet. It would be the devil of an afternoon. But secretly he loved the cold and dampness. It was not like years before when cold meant frozen handlebars on a bicycle and even colder knuckles to hold them. He thought, too, of the skimpy ragged clothes of those days—he had not owned a proper suit until Brendan had bought him one for his going away to the monastery. Thank God for comfort! He tucked his gloved hands into his fur-lined trench coat. He would walk home.

What an afternoon it had been! His nerves were raw from the noise of the classroom. There had been a time when he had assumed that the presence of books meant the presence of learning and wisdom. How wrong he had been. But he learned to cope with this letdown. He was convinced now that his own survival was the important thing. He dished out information. The students took it or left it. They did the work or they didn't. They passed the Leaving or failed. It was as simple as that. And the gaps in between afforded him the precious time to write and think—during his frequent exams, during his many worksheets, during his small-group discussions. Bless the Americans for their marvelous work-saving devices! Still, in the poll taken at Easter, he had been voted the most popular teacher on the staff, an honor envied by the other leather-and-stick teacher-at-the-head-of-the-room antiquarians. All he knew now was that he was glad to be outside the railings of the school for two short days. Two days of freedom from dissonance and ignorance. He felt like screaming or doing some wild thing. Instead, he crossed William Street. His sister, Josie, never remembered the newspaper on a Friday. She was too intent on getting home and washing herself for Seoirse Hayes. Big fat Seoirse. Colum would pick up the *Limerick Leader.*

He sighted the headlines long before he reached the stand:

MINISTER FOR JUSTICE WAYLAID IN SWAMP

PROUD AMBUSH SUSPECTED

He smiled to himself as he noticed the picture of Mulcahy on the front page. Lord, what an awful looking gawk! He had heard him on the radio. Seen him on the telly. Now, he looked like Farmer Murphy on his way to swill the pigs. But an ambush, dunking the old goat in a lot of mud and water, what did that accomplish? When was the organization going to get the style and arrogance of the Palestinians or the Israelis?

Colum wondered if Brendan had anything to do with this. Brendan Donnelly, the saboteur. The ambusher. The gunman. It didn't seem possible.

At the customhouse, he crossed to the shelter of Bank Place. He looked up at the clock. Five after five. By the time he'd eat his dinner and wash up it would be half past six. He'd never make the seven o'clock date with Ellen. Maybe he should call a Speedy Cab? Or wait for the next bus? To hell with it, he thought. A little inconvenience wasn't going to hurt her. It might do her good. He'd been too reliable, that was what he'd been.

When he reached College Park, the railway gates were closed against him. More delay. He decided to step into the gate box. The glow from the railway brazier would take the chill out of his wait.

Jimmy Byrnes, the gatekeeper, was huddled in the corner of the hut. "Awful day, Colum," he said without looking up.

"Yes. The town is in a flood."

"Ah, yes. But you're fine and secure in your schoolhouse. Central heat up to your arse."

"Ha."

" 'Tis well for you. Now if Robin Hood would take the same route . . ."

"Robin Hood?"

"Your brother. I calls him that. He's always on the go. Not time enough to piss straight. Where does he be going? I ask of you. He came through here not more than an hour ago and I swear to Jesus he nearly hit the four o'clock diesel to Ennis. A madman but a lovable one, God help us."

"Yes."

"Just like a big child."

The conversation was interrupted by the hoot of the train.

Through the window he could make it out as it crossed the Canal Bridge and rounded the bend by Jimmy Mulanney's farm. "A seaside train?" Colum asked.

"What else?"

"You're joking."

"A bunch of lads off to swim in the ocean and it the dead of winter still. Too much time and money they're given. Not an interest in anything but making fools of themselves."

When the trainload of boys flashed past the black and white gates, the occupants of the carriages hanging from the windows and waving furiously to all and everyone, Colum waved back. You were only young once, he thought with a certain nostalgia.

When Colum stepped through the gap, he noticed that Brendan's Morris Minor was parked near the shed. So the boyo was back from the wars. He was tempted to look inside the car, to find some clue to his brother's activities. But he didn't. His mother might be watching. The shock of knowing would be the death of her. He'd wait until later. He'd think of some excuse to get back outside.

In the kitchen, his mother was frying sausages. She looked up from the cooker as he entered. "Colum!" she said. "You're soaked!"

"I'm not."

"Why didn't you catch the bus?"

"I wanted to walk in the rain."

"Lord, amn't I scourged," she cried. "One likes to saunter in the rain, the other, inside in the bed, likes to travel up the country like a tinker or gypsy . . . "

So that had been Brendan's story, Colum thought. He turned to his mother. "Mama," he said, "I'm going to hang my topcoat up out in the shed and let some of the rain drip off it."

"All right. But come back in immediately. Your supper is almost ready. Don't you have a date with the Sullivan girl, too? You'd better hurry."

He didn't hear her last words as he covered his head with a newspaper and closed the door behind him. He sidled along the north wall. He looked towards his brother's window—the curtains were drawn. Now he was level with the car. He wiped the rain from the glass. There was nothing of interest inside. Some scattered road maps. An open pack of cigarettes. Maybe he had been wrong. Maybe Brendan *had* been working up the country.

It was then that the speedometer caught his eye. He remembered talking to his brother about the car's mileage not more than a week before on their way to twelve o'clock mass. He looked closely at the gauge. Aha! Not more than fifteen miles added since that time.

He stood back. It was possible after all. Brendan Donnelly. The fucker! The crazy mad mad fucker!

At the supper table, their mother's voice lashed over them as she ladled the sausages from the pan onto Colum's plate first and then Josie's. "My God," she said, "they're thundering villains. Imagine the cheek of it! Upsetting the Minister's car in broad daylight! Oh, we must be a show to the whole world, a laughingstock."

Colum turned his eyes in the direction of Brendan's bedroom. He hoped that his brother would stay there and not choose this moment to burst into the kitchen. He looked across at his sister. She carefully sliced the sausage on her plate but did not put it to her mouth.

The mother continued. "Bringing the war down from the North," she said, "instead of leaving it up there where it belongs. It's a different country up there—it might as well be Turkey or Egypt. Sure we never had anything in common with them. Even their names. They don't sound like our own, some of them. And Catholics? A fine Catholic their Devlin one was, with a bastard in her belly. And she as proud as Punch of it, mind you. Go on! It's easy to tell a hoodlum and a blackguard . . ."

Colum reached for the teapot and poured Josie a cup of

tea. He did not disagree with his mother. But neither did he agree with her allegiances. Boundaries. Creeds. Nationalities. Heroes. Villains. A cod, he thought. A great bloody cod.

Chapter 6

Brendan Donnelly awoke from his sleep. He had been dreaming of a strand somewhere on the west coast of Ireland. It had looked like Lahinch with the ragged cliffs to the south, but the strand was narrower and almost suffocated by the swelling sea. It was years before. Childhood. He could hear his father's voice calling out, "Jesus, Jesus, Colum is drownded!" And then the face of his brother appeared above the water, all blue and gouged, and like a reptile dredged up from the womb of the sea. It sneered back at him. Brendan cried out and ran to the water's edge. But the face disappeared below the green brine. He called out to his brother, "Colum, Colum!" There was only the echo of his voice as it darted across the water. Then he began to listen to the sound as it grew ever so faint. He called out again and thought that he saw the notes dance on the waves as they faded off towards Aran and Galway. He was caught by the diversion and forgot the face in the water and the hoarse cry of his father above on the stones.

The guilt of the dream would not leave him. He trembled in terror. His father's anniversary was not more than a week away. God love him, Brendan thought, and wished that the old man were near him now, to touch, to lean against, to see the eyes light up with laughter. The dream was surely a message, a plea for prayers. He must drop by the sacristy on his way uptown tonight. He'd have a few Masses said for his Da's soul.

And Colum's part in the dream, what did that mean? He couldn't make that out. He would ask one of the tinker women about it. They could read palms with frightening accuracy, why couldn't they give life to dreams? His mind drifted to Riordan's mention of Colum. He couldn't wait to tell the lad. If only he'd join the movement, if only they'd stand side by side as in years gone by, if only . . .

He looked up at the wall. He had pasted pictures of Pearse and Plunkett above that of the Sacred Heart. Below the holy picture, he had arranged in chronological order the speeches of the great patriots of the past. Wolfe Tone. Robert Emmett. Parnell.

He began to sing one of the old songs:

> Who fears to speak of '98,
> Who blushes at the name,
> When cowards mocked the patriot's fate,
> Who hanged his head for shame?
>
> He's all a knave or half a slave
> Who slights his country thus,
> But a true man, like you man,
> Will lift your glass with us.

He felt the fire mount inside him. Stupid fucking people! Electing castrated fools to be their leaders. Afraid of the bomb and the gas and the rubber bullet. Afraid of losing their comfort. What had happened to the greatness of the past? Fionn and his hurley? The Knights of the Red Branch? Conor Mac Neasa and the ball bursting from his royal head at the atrocity of the Saviour's death?

Then he remembered what he had seen that afternoon from his car. Four Hare Krishna maniacs dancing and ringing bells outside Todd's. And behind them, scratched on the wall, the words:

ABORTION IS CHILD'S PLAY

He put his head down on the pillow and wept bitterly.

Chapter 7

Whaen Colum stepped off the Corbally bus, he saw Ellen Sullivan standing in the archway to Todd's Stores. She seemed so small, so insignificant, there in the shadows. Twenty past seven. He shouldn't have been late.

Ellen saw him and her face lit up. "Colum," she said, "I thought you were never coming!"

"I left school late," he said. "And then I had to walk home. I missed the bus."

She pressed against his arm. "Lord," she said, "I was in dread of my life. Two drunkards were standing against the outside window arguing. One had put a lighted match in the other's shoe, then kicked him in the shins. And hippies, the place is swarming with them. I don't know what this town is coming to at all."

"They wouldn't have harmed you. They're just small nuisances. Forget about them. Where do you want to go, to the pictures?"

"It's all the one to me, Colum. We've seen most of them, though. What about that group from the Gaeltacht that's at Driscoll's? I hear they're terribly good. We could catch the bus out, if you'd like."

"No," he said crossly. "I'm tired of that traditional la-di-da. Isn't it bad enough that we're bombarded with it every day and night on RTE without sitting and hearing an earful of it for money? Let's go to the Carlton. There's a good American one on there. I heard one of the older lads talking about it today."

"It's X-rated."

"So? Are we children that we can't stand a bit of sex? We might learn something."

Ellen remained silent. Her arm still rested in his, and she allowed herself to be led across O'Connell Street.

The queue outside the Carlton was slight. There would be even fewer inside. He and Ellen would have the balcony to themselves, he thought. This cheered him. A good court on a rainy night was just the cure. He leaned in front of her to pay for the tickets.

He had been right. The expensive balcony seats were empty except for an older lady who seemed to be dozing in the lower corner. He and Ellen climbed the steps to the back row. The picture was beginning. The sounds of clashing cymbals. The peal of trumpets. The roar of racing cars as they thundered across the screen and then disappeared.

Ellen put her hand in his and rested her dark head on his shoulder. He sank into the seat and glanced up at the credits. Nobody they recognized. No James Stewarts. No John Waynes. No Burt Lancasters. Just a list of half-French, half-German, half-Oriental names. He had made a good choice.

He kissed her neck. She responded by moving her face in his direction. He could feel her breasts now against his chest and the light scent of her perfume in his nostrils. He was aware of his rising excitement, and he cursed the awkwardness of his body. But Ellen hadn't seemed to notice.

He leaned back against the seat. He was nearing the limit of their intimacy. A few heated caresses. A pressing here and there. A pause. And then the renewal of the impotent ritual again. The same old story, the same old rules of the game played so close to home and hearth.

Behind them he noticed the flickering of the projector beam. Disparate shafts of light brought to fullness on the screen. Scattered parts made into a whole. And yet below him in the brightness they fell into characters and objects of pure sterility. How much more important than the sum were the fractions? And the precepts that held him back, that curbed his natural instincts, how intrinsic were they to the life beyond the cloister and his own parish, to the life of the now sprawling city with its nameless faces and far-flung townships? They were meaningless except to those within the pale. He thought of his brother and his possible connection to the ambush that morning. In a week it would all be forgotten, and new adventures and atrocities would have to replace it. But the fact that Brendan had been involved, had celebrated its violence, was important. Was vital.

He lifted the edge of Ellen's blouse and touched the warm flesh of her back. She moaned softly. He moved his hand to her breast and, though she twisted to avoid his touch, he knew that she was responding to his ploy. For a second he hesitated, but he purged himself of the indecision. He stroked the ruffled texture of her brassiere.

Suddenly, Ellen grasped his hand. "No, Colum, don't," she said. "Please don't."

"Why not?"

"You know why. We have no right."

"We have every right. It seems to me that you were enjoying the hell out of it, just as I was."

"Would I be human if I didn't? But I'm not an animal of the field . . ."

"Here we go with the sermons. Ellen Sullivan, the first Retreat Mistress!"

"That's enough. I'm leaving." She reached for her coat. The old lady below them had heard their voices and was looking about. Colum sank into the seat.

"Let me out," Ellen said. "There's no talking to you. Something's inside of you tonight."

She brushed past his knees and cautiously descended the narrow steps. For a moment she seemed to pause but then hurriedly turned the corner of the passageway.

On the screen, a racing car crashed into the stands leveling several barricades and strewing bodies this way and that. He heard the old lady cry out in a clear voice, "Oh, Jesus, have mercy on us!"

Chapter 8

Colum Donnelly left the Carlton Cinema long after the picture had ended and the late house began. Outside the weather had softened and he felt a warm breeze from the docks touch his face. It was early, only ten o'clock. Perhaps he should take a stroll down by Harvey's Quay. It might do him good.

He wondered about Ellen. Had she caught the bus home? A tension came into him as he thought of the drunkards and the hippies of the early evening. He shouldn't have let her walk up there by herself. But she'd asked for it. He hadn't expected her to react so decisively over such a trifle. You'd swear that he had tried to rob her of her virginity. God, Jesus!

He was tired of being told what to do, advised, given counsel. He was his own man. Hadn't he chosen to become a Brother, secured for himself a good education, faced the gawking mouths when he returned home without the half-collar? The rhetoric with himself stirred his blood. He felt for a moment that he was part of a scene, an actor being as brave or as callous as the part demanded. He looked down at his polished shoes, the neatly pressed trousers, the well-made topcoat. He told himself that he was a man of stature, a cut above the rest. He stiffened at the thought.

As he crossed Bedford Row, a car skidded to avoid him. He jumped quickly to the footpath and looked back. The driver shouted, "You stupid bastard! Dreaming in the middle of the road . . ."

"Up yours!"

A head popped out of the front window. "Shit! If it isn't my ejamicated brother!"

Colum recognized the familiar slur of the words. His brother had more than a few pints in. Celebrating his grand accomplishment of the morning, no doubt. "Well," he responded, "our brave I.R.A. gunman. Mr. Patrick Mulcahy's nemesis. The brave boyo . . ."

The other was out of the car. "Colum, will you shut your bloody mouth? You'll have the Guards on us in a minute."

The two men faced each other. They stood almost equal in height, though Brendan was more sturdily built than his brother. His face, too, was different. In a crowd of a thousand, he would be easily marked as "Irish." The ruddy complexion, the fair hair, the blue eyes, the uneven teeth. Colum, on the other hand, might be mistaken for a foreigner. Italian, maybe. Or French. Everything about him was dark. There was added to that the air of the ascetic.

"Where's the bird?" Brendan asked.

"Flown."

"So early? What did you do? Try to tickle her under her knickers?"

"As a matter of fact . . ."

"You randy fucker! Miracles will never cease. I didn't know you had it in you, boy!"

"You never know what lurks in the soul of man."

Brendan's face brightened. He scratched his cheek. "Where are you off to now?" he asked. "To commit suicide?"

"In my arse."

"Well, get in. Look out there over Clare. It'll be pissing again soon."

"Where are you off to? Another ambush?"

"Will you get the fuck in or not? We're going out for a bash. You're welcome if you want to come."

"Who's 'we'?"

"Liam Daly. And the girls in the back—Maevis, Deirdre, and Rayana."

"Rayana?"

"Some Yank bitch. Over here to spend her bucks and see the peasants trudge their way to freedom from blood-sodden fields."

"Jesus, you're mad." Some of the awe with which he had regarded Brendan, as a schoolboy, was now infecting him again, despite his efforts to control it. "I'll go along," he said.

Colum stooped to enter. Daly nodded respectfully. "Hello,

Colum," he said. Donnelly recognized the face from his secondary school days. A mediocre student who quit after his Intermediate. The girls smiled. They were pleased to meet any brother of Brendan's. He was a card, they said. Could there possibly be two of him? Colum wondered if he should have come.

The American did not speak until he settled himself beside her. Then she said, "You're a high school teacher?"

"Secondary. Who said?"

"Your brother, earlier."

"Ah, yes."

"What major?"

"Subject? English."

"The same as myself. I taught elementary school in Waukegan, Illinois, when I first graduated."

"And now?"

"I'm on a sabbatical leave. No job, no worries, nothing."

"Are you staying with relatives?"

"No. I'm at the George Hotel. I love it. So quaint."

"It is that. English plumbing."

"Ha."

Brendan made the formal introductions as he rammed the car into gear and crossed Sarsfield Street on a yellow light. Maevis was a secretary for one of the Societies. Deirdre worked for An Bord Failte, the tourist agency. And, of course, Rayana. But Colum and she were great friends already, he said, so there was no need for the bother of introduction. Though embarrassed, Colum removed his glove, extended his hand, and said, "Very pleased, I'm sure."

When she returned his gesture, he noticed that her hands were soft, unused to the likes of bleach and soda. He had written a story once of a girl whose hands were coarse and crusted. In the fiction, she had kept them gloved always for fear that they might infect, on touch, the soft flesh of the rest of her body. He forgot the outcome. Rayana wore a ring on her small finger. Part of its mounting was broken and scratched his finger. But he pretended not to notice.

Their destination turned out to be Langer's pub on Wolfe

Tone Street, halfway between the home of the Redemptorist Confraternity, to the south, and the whorehouses of the lower docks, to the west. Colum, before entering the monastery, had been very conscious of this truce line and had often drawn sketches of the polarities that tore at its center. On many nights, after Benediction at the Confraternity, he had stood on O'Connell Avenue and looked with interest at the brown building with its Players and Woodbine signs. He had wondered then what people frequented the inside. Priests on the lookout for lost souls? Prostitutes offering their wares to the sanctimonious? But the novitiate had rid him of such speculation. Sin, once named, examined, broken into its stages, seemed to lose a measure of its awe. Masturbation, sodomy, and adultery were diminished somewhat by the mere act of being described.

He might have guessed—Langer's pub was no different from those in his own parish. Glasses piled on trays. Mirrors. Sawdust on the floor. A few Guinness barrels for atmosphere. A sign that read: "Toilets Out Back." He glanced at the clientele. A man and a woman in their sixties. Two tweedy girls sipping on cordials. A few wild-looking teenagers debating some loud issue in the back.

Brendan and Liam Daly pushed several of the red barrels together as the girls excused themselves to the toilets. Colum searched about for an extra chair. When he finally returned with a small stool, Brendan said, "We're not matched up. Deirdre and her pal are two dead rides—I know. But I'm not sure about the Yank. One of the other ones insisted that we take her along. Seems that they met her at the Green Hills or the Motel or someplace. So which one of them do you want to jag with, Colum?"

"Ask Liam first."

"It's all the one with me," Liam said. "I'll take Maevis, if you like."

Colum felt relief. He somehow had anticipated that Liam might choose Rayana. Now it was decided. Brendan would never match himself with the Yank.

"That settles it," his brother said. "I'll take Deirdre."

The girls were back. Drinks were ordered and delivered. "Up the Republic!" Brendan said as he raised his glass.

"Up the Republic!"

Colum remained silent. He looked at Rayana. Her small dark eyes seemed to devour each detail of the ritual. It was as though she had heard a secret formula or code and had immediately set about deciphering it. She was staring now at Brendan, anticipating his next move. He made it by standing tall and saying, "Breathes there a man with soul so dead, who never to himself hath said, 'This is my own, my native land!' "

The others in the pub paid little attention but went on about their business. Colum saw Brendan's eyes take in the full room as he added, "An end to tyranny and oppression." But still, all that was elicited was the barest glance from one of the tweedy girls.

Rayana touched Colum's arm. "I hear that your brother is an important man in the I.R.A.," she whispered.

"Who said that?"

"The boy with him. Dalton?"

"Daly."

"Though I don't agree with their cause, I think it's exciting. My brothers are all into the movement in the States. Last year, they raised thirty thousand dollars for arms to be smuggled here. Their Irish Club's fund-raising is more successful than the Bishop's Relief Drive."

"You're Catholic?"

"With a name like Duggan?"

"But . . ."

"My Christian name?"

"Yes."

"Rayana. It's the de-virginized version of Anne—Anne Brigid Duggan."

He smiled. Her words seemed brash and not in taste. Yet she had uttered them with a certain ease, a casualness that would have been lost on the lips of the other girls. What was it that Joyce had said of American girls? ". . . unkempt, fierce, and beautiful." Rayana was not quite that. But as he put his eyes on her, he observed the tousled arrangement of her hair, the open blouse, the slightest glimpse of the colored under-things. A wave of sensual enjoyment, such as he had never experienced with Ellen or others, went through him. He was reminded of the days when he'd first come home on holiday from the monastery and had strolled out each afternoon by the Baths in Corbally. How he had tried to keep his eyes on the river but had failed time and time again, allowing them to stray to the pinks and whites and blues of the girls' clothing on the riverbank. How he had recited aspiration after aspiration to no avail. How he had been disappointed that his black suit and half-collar had not protected him from the world of summer excitement all about. This time he took pleasure in his reverie and felt no remorse.

Brendan had begun to sing "The Green Boys" in a reedy tenor voice. Colum looked up at the embarrassing figure. What had separated their ways and spun them miles apart? The Primary Certificate—a mere examination of childhood that Brendan had failed by a few meager points, an event which had condemned him to the wasteland of vocational school. Colum had passed with honors when his time came, a result of constant study of the old tests. The practice had been forbidden by the headmaster of Brendan's days. A fluke, in a way. And this was one of the results. Colum had to remind himself of his affection for the great oaf.

"Where did you take your degree?" Rayana said, losing interest in the spectacle.

He pretended not to have heard. But she persisted. "Trinity? National University?"

"Teachers' college. They sent me there."

" 'They'?"

"The Brothers. I was in their novitiate until recently."

"I'm sorry. I didn't mean to pry."

"It's all right. I'm free of the whole mess now."

"My brother was a Franciscan monk for a while. He's now a porno vendor in Los Angeles! What a trip! From visions to inserts in three short years. The rest of the family won't have a thing to do with him, the hypocrites. He says that he came in contact with more weirdos then than he does now. You'll have to tell me about your experiences, sometime."

"I will."

"It's a date." She leaned over and pressed his arm.

Around them the song had changed to discussion of the North. Maevis was questioning Brendan. "How do you propose to bring all this reform about?" she asked.

"Nothing simpler. It's just a matter of getting the power out of the hands of the eejits in the Dail. If it wasn't for them, the whole question would be settled in a month."

"What are they doing wrong?"

"They're feathering their own beds. Mulcahy. Roche. Moynihan. The whole bloody lot. They don't care what happens to the workingman in the South, or to the misfortune who hasn't held two days of work together in his life up North. It's a conspiracy."

"A conspiracy?"

"Yes. Between the fuckers in Westminster and our own bloodsuckers in Leinster House. Why should any of them worry? Their arses are warm. Their children go to private schools."

"But what's to be done?"

"Everything must be torn from its roots and hurled skywards and must fall like rain in the fields of simple men. The whole country must be dismantled and united under the flag of a truly republican and free Ireland."

His voice was like that of an Old Testament prophet, and Colum was frightened by the sheer authority of it. It reminded him of their dead father's incomprehensible rages, so often directed at himself. He was startled when Rayana interrupted.

"But Brendan," she said, "why is it that Southern Ireland is now enjoying more prosperity than it ever has—cars, entertainment, goods in the store, membership in the Common Market . . ."

"Horseshit! That's what you Americans would like to think. You come over here with your bloody cameras and microphones. You take a few pictures and then it's off with you again. And you talk about a 'religious war' and what a strange primitive out-of-time thing it is. You don't know 'A' from a bull's bollicks about one thing in the world besides your own sterile lifeless country. You know nothing of heart. And you have tried to infect the world with your disease. We have heart here in Ireland, by God, though I'll admit it's fast fading. But we'll have it 'beat loud with joy' again very soon . . ."

Colum's hand shook as he lifted his coat from the chair and stood up. He detested this venom-in-the-face approach so often exerted by his brother. He was a fool to have thought that there was an iota left of their past camaraderie. "Goodnight, all," he said and turned to leave.

"Stay awhile, won't you?" Brendan said softly. Then with a sudden bitterness in his voice he continued, "You might learn a little more about the truth than you'll find in your fancy books."

Once outside, Colum turned north towards home. His brother's insult hung in his mind. He knew the well of despair and ignorance from which it had arisen, and he declared himself the victor. His silence and indifference would torment Brendan more than any argument. He had often used the same ploy on their father. He sighed with pleasure as he touched the garden railings along O'Connell Avenue and allowed his fingertips to feel the dry crusted paint.

"Colum! Colum!" The voice startled him. He turned to see the slender figure of Rayana cross the wet street.

"Hello, again," he said. "You'll have pneumonia tomorrow from this wringing air."

"That's all right. I just wanted to catch you before you were swallowed up by the city."

He looked into her face. Beneath the gas light she seemed more attractive than before. Like an actress, he thought.

Some American actress he remembered from a film now long forgotten. It was the symmetry of her features as the stark shadows played on their contours. The lips, the eyes, the skin. All combining to form a set perfection. He thought of Ellen. Rayana was not like her in any way. None of the schoolgirl freckles, none of the rough scrubbed skin, none of the tendency towards overweight. "I'm sorry," he said. "Sorry about Brendan. He's impossible, at times. There's no talking to him."

"You shouldn't have left on my account. Blood is thicker than . . ."

"Water."

"Yes."

"No. No. There's little between my brother and myself."

Standing in the rain, he sensed suddenly his own lack of importance, his inability to separate himself from the stagnation all about him. What had the argument with Ellen proved? Or the incident with his brother? And yet in some way they had created a demand, an imperative that nagged him and seemed to say, "Do more. Do more. Let the gears mesh." He looked at his companion from across the world. To merely walk with her through the streets would be enough. To defy the rain and the gawking eyes and the prospect of rumor in this city of rumors. He said with trepidation, "Might I buy you a drink somewhere? Your own hotel, maybe?"

"Fine. Are we far from there? I'm lost in this town!"

It had all been so simple, so much like child's play. "Far?" he said. "Oh, no. Not far at all."

Without warning, she linked her arm in his. A tension took hold of him. But he told it to be still and allowed the natural peace of the night and the airy briskness of their walk to untangle it.

Chapter 9

The vestibule of the George was deserted except for the night receptionist who dozed behind the glass panes of the counter. At their entrance, he shook himself and said, "Good evening. Dreadful weather, Miss Duggan."

"Yes," she replied. And turning to Colum, she whispered, "I tipped him well when I arrived. My old man used to always say that the quickest way to a man's heart was through his pocket."

As they turned into the hallway, the sound of piano music greeted them from the lounge bar. They stood for a moment listening to the languorous strains, then in silent agreement faced into this late-hour melody.

The lounge was not crowded. A few faces looked up in their direction as they entered but turned again into the darkness. Colum pointed to a lighted table at the far end of the room. "That one's close to the bar," he explained. "We won't lack for service."

When the drinks were delivered, Rayana lifted the shamrock-emblazoned glass and said, "Here's to seeing more of each other."

"I'll drink to that notion and to the clearing of the weather . . ."

"Oh, no. I love this rain. I think it makes for the 'real' Ireland, the place where towering imaginations are bred, where violent poets scourge out their imagery . . . " She laughed.

Colum was not sure how to take her remarks. He said, " 'Now Ireland has her madness and her weather still.' "

"Joyce."

"Auden on Yeats."

"Oh, yes."

"Yeats lived near here at one time. A few miles up country. Kilfenora Castle."

"He *did?* I'll have to take that in. I couldn't return to my

literary friends without that to my credit. Is it obscure? I
mean, do many know of it?"

"Well, it's out of the way. Few pay attention to it. Most are
concerned with the Sligo area."

"Great!"

"There are other interesting places."

"Oh, I'll have to take them all in. It's a must."

"That might be impossible."

"Not in a month, surely?"

"Well . . ." He thanked God Brendan was not here—he'd
skin her alive. Colum, too, might have felt irritated, but what
had she said that would have warranted this? That Ireland, to
her, was nothing more than a national park with graves and
shrines and medieval castles in place of geysers and bears?
The idea intrigued him. It was as though he viewed this
pitiable island from a great height, and by reason of his
perspective, controlled it. Of course, it was an illusion, but it
was one that produced a real effect.

Minutes later she had finished her whiskey. He made to
order another, but she refused. "I have to be up early," she
said. "I'm to pick up a car at Dan Ryan's."

"Punch's Cross?"

"Yes. That's the place."

"It's south of here. You catch the bus outside of Woolworth's—the other side of the street."

Suddenly, she said, "Listen. I've got a great idea—why
don't *you* come along? We can spend the whole day . . ."

He surprised himself when he said, "What time?"

"Nine."

"Nine it is."

"Here."

"Here."

There. It was done. And all as simple as crossing your
fingers.

Chapter 10

When Colum unlatched the kitchen door, he was aware immediately of someone watching him from behind the glare of the fire. "Josie? Seoirse?" he called.

But there was no answer. A shiver went through him, but he told himself that there was nothing to be afraid of. Had he been a child once again, he might have entertained the notion of a ghost's presence, his father's, maybe. But he had put such excuses out of his mind years ago. He had forced himself free of them by walking through the churchyard at the novitiate in the dead of night and concentrating on the vision of the bodies rising out of their narrow cells. He had met no one worse than himself. He reasoned that his fear now was nothing more than a curiosity for the unknown. He said, "Mama?"

"It's me, damn it! You'll wake the whole fucking house. Who'd you think I was, the banshee?"

"No."

"Who then?"

"Fat Seoirse Hayes, maybe."

"Lord, aren't we the proud ones. The Donnelly name standing high above all the other poor yobs. Seoirse is like one of our own. He's parish."

"But he's not one of our own. Seoirse with breasts on him like an old woman. Sniffing around Josie . . ."

"Jesus, he might not be the best-looking creature on the earth. But he's got tons of nature. What more could our 'gorgeous' sister ask for? When was it that good looks made happiness?"

"Oh, not this idiocy . . ."

"All right. Truce. Tell me, how did you get on with your Yank? I saw you leave the George."

"You saw me leave the George and you didn't stop to give me a lift?"

"Well, I thought you needed a little cooling down. Why with all that hot stuff on your hands . . ."

"Fuck off!"

"Aha!" Brendan's laugh was hearty and it infected his brother. They joined together in its release.

"You're lucky Ellen didn't see you."

"To hell with her. She's an old maid. I've turned over a new leaf."

"Nookey for breakfast, dinner, and supper."

"I wouldn't turn my nose up at it."

"An ex-monk and mad for his iron."

"Talk to me tomorrow—I'm taking Rayana up to Kilfenora."

"What?"

"Yes. We're going to look at the Yeats tower."

"But you're not going to be seen in the day with her?"

"Why not? She's a girl—and a good-looking one at that. What's the matter? I've been half dead long enough. You said so yourself, tonight."

Brendan put his hand on his brother's shoulder. "Colum," he said, "I didn't mean a word of it. I was just pissed at the Yank. They know everything. If they see it, they own its very soul—or so they think."

"No. It's true about me. I need to know the world I live in. The real world outside the walls. I need to explore."

"But explore the place about you first, slowly and surely. Otherwise, you'll be confused. You'll be seeing everything with a monk's eye, thinking that the world is as manageable as a postage stamp."

"No. I must cross the safe cozy bar . . ."

"Sure, if it's adventure you want, or a bit of the gay-box . . ."

"You don't understand. My whole bloody life is as dependable as a cant. Monk. Ex-monk. Eternal bachelor or modest husband. Can't you see?"

"No . . . "

"Even if I were a homosexual—it would be something

bizarre, something to stir me to life, to cause a little trouble."

"Don't say that, Colum."

"I will. It's true. Brother Grady, the old bent queer, gets more out of life than I do, I swear to God. This girl that you're worried about, this Rayana, she's seen the world. She knows what's out there beyond the Clare Hills."

He put his face in his hands, and in that instant he recognized the effect on his brother. Had he become entranced by his own rhetoric? Was his heart a footstep behind his words? But to use the proper choice of words was not a deceit. Was it? It was a rule . . .

Before he had a chance to consider his motives further, Brendan grasped him about the neck in a strong but friendly grip. "Listen, Colum," he said, "I have the answer for you. I have the doorway out."

The movement, Colum thought. He should not have opened up to Brendan. He should have anticipated that it would lead to this, a circus in a saucer, with this great child across from him as ringmaster. What had gotten into him? The only solution was to play along. "What is that?" he said.

"I have someone that's interested in you, in your writing."

"Who? Some whore?"

"No. No."

"Who, then?"

"You'd never guess in all your born days."

"Quit with the game. One of your boyo friends who . . ."

"Ah, yes. The boyo of boyos—Taig Riordan himself."

"What?"

"Himself!"

" 'The Renegade'?"

"The very one."

"You're joking."

"I'm as serious as death."

Colum was genuinely awed by the revelation. Taig Riordan, the mystery man of the movement. Another De Valera. Born in the States. Educated at Oxford. And now the brilliant new intelligence behind much of the surreptitious activities in the South. His name was on every tongue that spoke with grudging praise of the Provos. Take it away and what had you left? A bunch of illiterates and blackguards, the dregs on which the I.R.A. fed until he arrived on the scene. Colum remembered when this man had been imprisoned, and he recalled the outcry that had ensued.

Brendan was on fire. "I spoke to him today, this very day."

"In Limerick?"

"In Laffey's pub. We had other business, but he came back to you again and again. He's a fan of yours—the stories in *The Press* and *The Times*."

"He liked them?"

"Was mad out about them. Said that you were a smart man."

"Ah, go away!"

"Said that I ought to try and convert you."

"There's no fear of that, I'm afraid."

"You have no love for the country that gave you life . . ."

"Jesus, don't start that again! I have love for me. For Mama, Josie, and yourself. Fuck all else."

Brendan, like a scolded child, fell into silence. He raised the iron poker and stirred the ashes of the fire.

Colum was aware of the blow he had dealt his brother. But he had told the truth. Still, maybe he should have put it in a different way. "Listen," he said. "Our values are as different as chalk and cheese—there's no changing that. I'm never going to be the patriot that you are, so let's leave that side of it out, once and for all. But to be honest with you, I wouldn't mind meeting 'The Renegade' sometime. I might get a story out of it, you'd never know."

Brendan came back to life. "You'd do that?"

"Why not?"

"I know I could arrange it."

"Fine. And now I'm off to bed. I have to be up early."

"Goodnight."

" 'Night."

Colum closed the door behind him and left his brother in the faint red glow from the fire. The figure reminded him of Kitty the Hare, the character in the schoolboy papers of long ago. Huddled up against the embers as though the wind and the rain might suddenly send them pell-mell into the night.

Chapter 11

The sun was climbing the sills and walls as Colum entered Lock Quay. It was a relief to be out from under the rain, he thought. He looked at his watch. Half eight. He'd have time for an expresso at the Capri before picking up Rayana. That would make him a minute or so late. But he wanted that. No point in giving the impression that he was an over-eager native, was there?

Once in the restaurant, he sat back against the leather cushions of the booth and slowly sipped the thick creamy coffee. How good it was to be alive. To be free of encumbrances. To be a thing of sail and not harbor. Looking at the street beyond the window, he watched the girls in their cotton dresses walk daintily into the sunshine from the shadows of his side of the street, the housewives jig their wicker baskets as though they were appendages of their own bodies, the older women draw their shawls about them, afraid of the newness of the warmth, terrified that it might give them their deaths. And he imagined that he was part and parcel of them all, that he had entered into a communion with these early risers.

Suddenly, his attention was captured by the sight of two great horses that burst upon his vision. Behind them they drew a black hearse, decorated in the colors of the Republic. The funeral of an old soldier. Brendan would get a mile out of this, he thought.

And as he had become one with the life of the street a second before, he felt compelled to enter upon the experience of the black cortege. Old men behind the hearse. Old friends waiting out their own time. Old women on the footpath watching their spouses and brothers. He had never looked at death objectively. In the novitiate, he had examined the circumstances of death. Entering death in doubt, in grace, in sin. But it had been an unheeded specter, so far removed and isolated from the young black-garbed postulants. Death stood for incense, requiem Masses, the Lazarus gospel. Even at the funeral of his father he had not looked death in the eye. (He remembered his guilt at having wondered if his collar were straight during the graveside services.) He had seen his father's death in terms of his own loss. On this April morning, he felt a strange sensation take hold of him. He imagined that he looked out through the eyes of the dead peasant in the glass hearse and saw the people all about like dolled-up chimpanzees. He saw the laws of this land, the covenants, the moralities built on shame and praise, the very perfumes and ointments in the chemists' windows, all, all of them hedges against the jungle and the inevitable clutch of this last day. He shuddered. He forced his eyes away from the scene outside and focused his attention on the ice-cream dish painted on the sign above him. He read over and over the words printed at its base: "Tantalizes the palate into ecstasies of pure pleasure."

He paid his bill. The funeral had passed, and the town had taken on again the warm full-of-life attitude of a few minutes before.

Rayana was waiting for him in the vestibule of the hotel. Her hair was tied neatly behind her head in a tight ponytail. She smiled the white smile as he came through the doorway. She made no mention of his lateness. "I'm all ready," she said. "Ready to see the sights." Without warning, she leaned over and kissed him on the lips.

Several old women on their way to morning Mass paused and looked in upon them. Colum thought that he recognized one of them. Bridie what's-her-name? He turned back to Rayana and pressed his lips on hers.

Chapter 12

Brendan Donnelly stood outside the Labor Exchange and searched in his pocket for his unemployment cards. It was nearly nine o'clock. He had been up for over an hour and yet the sleep of the bed was still on him. He had hoped that he would have a word with Colum, before the lad left, but when he'd come out into the kitchen, the bugger was gone, gone off to the countryside with a Yank half-whore.

Passing under the archway of the government office, he heard the familiar lingo of the unemployed. "Trixie Clover" in the fourth. "Orange Pip" in the sixth. Three to one. To win. To place. He smiled. Thank God he hadn't acquired *that* bad habit. He had enough others. And it was on the increase lately. Did they ever bring a penny home to their families? Corruption everywhere.

He reached the pay window and signed the usual cards. The clerk looked up from the page before him but said nothing.

"Raef," Brendan said, "how's tricks?"

"Tricks? Haven't you heard?"

"Heard what?"

"About the lads?"

"What about the lads? What lads?"

A man came up behind. Raef Buckley handed Brendan a form and said, "Report to Mossie Reedy's Coalyard in Market Place. If you do, you'll get a day's labor. Fill that out before you go." He turned to the next customer. "Morning. Lovely day."

The man filled in his daily card and left the window. He had been merely a regular, eager to get his name on paper, lay claim to a few meager pounds, and be on his way again to the gambling school outside.

Brendan was back. "Speak, man," he said.

Buckley whispered his words. "Arrested," he said. "Fifteen lads from the parish. Picked up by the Guards in the middle of the fucking night. Like sheep."

"Who?"

"Two that were with you yesterday—Duff and Ryan."

"Daly?"

"No. They didn't touch him. But there were others. Nearly all of the active lads in the parish, the ones they suspect but have no proof on. It's a bit strange, isn't it?"

"It's funny that they didn't look me up. I'm in the parish, too."

"You are?"

"Sure. Park was added to St. Mary's a few years back."

"Go on. I'll bet you few people know that."

"Back to the lads—where are they holding them?"

"In William Street Barracks."

"Bloody bastards, imprisoning their own kind."

"True. But Brendie, for God's sake watch your step. They may know more than we give them credit for. It may be a setup of some sort. Don't do anything rash . . ."

Without further conversation, Brendan turned on his heel and left the Labor Exchange. He ignored the pleas of the backers and gamblers to join them in their uncertain sport. But one face caught his eye. It was that of a young fellow he had worked with on the docks. The boy was now counting out his change on the fringe of the crowd. "Jamesie," Brendan said, "I thought you got into Spaights?"

"I did."

"What are you doing here with this bunch of knackers?"

"Placing a few shillings . . ."

"But the job?"

"Ah, I chucked it."

"What?"

"Ara, bad 'cess to work when you can get nearly as much

on the dole. Why strain yourself? Enjoy the welfare state is what I says."

By the time he reached William Street, the sky had darkened. Great clouds were drifting up from the mouth of the Shannon, and he knew that the heavens would open any minute. Already he could feel the drops against his cheeks. He stood outside the Barracks' gate. He only wished that it were possible to tear the iron barricades asunder and to give these country-mug Guards the hiding of their lives. He almost felt like marching in there and shouting in their faces, "I'm your man, you pack of bollicks. Deal with me, not with these lads." But he knew that this would accomplish little. It would only serve to assure the Guards that their suspicions were correct and to hand them on a platter the goose as well as the eggs.

He'd hold off a bit before doing anything. Riordan would have the situation well in hand, if he knew him.

Chapter 13

Kilfendora Castle was a disappointment to Rayana, and she did not hesitate to say so. She had expected something more in line with the power and majesty of Yeats, more aristocratic, more renowned. Instead, she found a dilapidated, moss-covered old ruin, full of weeds and vermin and cow manure. Why hadn't the Bord Failte improved this place as they had other shrines and landmarks? Did the Irish have something against their great poets?

"But he wasn't Irish," Colum said coyly.

"What?"

"He wasn't. He was of English stock—born in the Pale, as we say. He was always a foreigner, here. Very much like Shaw—another *Sasanach*. Do you know that before a few years ago, I knew only one poem by Yeats—'Lake Isle of Innisfree.' And I thought, then, in my foolishness, that it was lousy poetry."

"Why?"

"It didn't have a regular rhyme pattern."

"Oh, Jesus—a lot of chance Creeley or Plath would have here."

"None at all. Let it rhyme or let it die, that's our motto."

"Our?"

"Our country's."

"Ha."

Colum had lost some of his reserve with her. In the light of day, he found her to be audacious, inclined to small imperfections and annoyances. But he liked her forthrightness, that American quality of saying what was on the tongue. So unlike here, he thought, where the word is only half of it, the sting coming hours later when you are miles away. Her way courted rebuff, of course, but when it was all over, there was little to mull about. He imitated her brashness when he said, "Let's forget hunting relics and have supper in Ennis."

She smiled. "You've read my mind," she said. "I'm sorry about being disappointed in the cow pastures and stinky old gravesides. They remind me of the tomb, and that's a dull prospect. It all seemed so romantic when you spoke about it last night."

"Brendan might disagree with us and call us traitors."

"He might have us shot!"

"Don't count *against* that."

It was not right to be talking about his own flesh and blood like this. But what harm? It was only a joke.

They arrived back in Limerick about eight o'clock and parked the rented American Ford in the hotel yard off Henry Street. The rain was falling heavily now, making it madness to venture towards the main building without an umbrella.

Instead, they sat in the spacious car, the engine running, the radio playing a Dylan song, the air outside turning unseasonably cold.

"Well," Rayana said, "I had a delightful day. I'm sorry . . ."

"That's all right. I understand."

Rayana made no response but leaned across the seat and kissed him. Her tongue entered his mouth. He found himself taken unawares, unable to muster his thoughts for the moment. He was terrified. He remembered her caustic remarks on those in religion. He must not be grouped with them or with the fumbling lads of his classroom. Gaining his senses, he steadied himself against the door. It became clear to him what he must do to satisfy. Slowly he manipulated his own tongue in the snakelike ritual. She moaned and seemed lost to his very presence. She reminded him of animals he had seen in the hot haze of day, their gazes fixed on some object far off on the horizon.

His success obvious, he moved his hand to her thighs and began a methodical back and forward motion of his palm. (He had seen an illustration of this in a sex primer confiscated from one of the desks in his room and ordered destroyed by Headmaster. He had read it carefully before tossing it into the furnace.) Rayana's body writhed, and her breathing became more hurried. He searched, as though locating terrain on a map, and found the private place and stroked the damp flesh. He was master of this Rayana, this foreign girl, so recently arrogant and independent. His sexual excitement was great, but he strived through the diversion of his thoughts to the green light of the radio, the hum of the motor, and a myriad other things within his radius, to keep the explosion of pleasure stayed for the few moments longer. It had worked in dreams, it must work here, he told himself.

But before he could divert his thoughts further, Rayana seemed to suddenly awaken from her stupor. She looked up at him with clear eyes. Reaching down, she grasped him through the heavy cloth of his trousers. It was as though her fingernails bit through the fabric. And she relieved him of his long-stayed seed. Almost casually she said, "I'm sorry. But this is not the right day."

Then, her expression changing, she exclaimed, "You little bastard. The Brothers never hurt you!" With that, she bit him inside his collar. He jumped back in pain. His hand touched his neck. She had broken the skin, and his fingers were wet with blood. But he could not be angry with her. He delighted in the utter insanity of what she had done.

Now she had to go on up, she said. A friend was coming by tomorrow. They were driving down country to see Blarney Castle. But she'd be back by nightfall. She would see him then.

He chose to remain in the car a while longer as there seemed to be no letting up in the rain.

Chapter 14

Seoirse Hayes shifted his large frame in the armchair and said, "Jesus, me leg is asleep. Will you get up a minute, Josie, love, and let it come back to life."

Josie moved off his lap. "Are you sure it's your leg?"

"Ah, it's a dead cert," he replied, not catching her joke. He limped about the Donnelly kitchen like a great elk in calf, grasping his knee as he moved.

Brendan was seated at the kitchen table. He paid little attention to the activity but instead scoured the night's papers for any word of the arrested men. But there was none.

"Brendie," Seoirse called to him. "We're going to run on in to Paddy-Whack at the Cosy for a few bags of fish and chips. Can we bring you back some?"

"No. Thanks. I'll be off to bed soon."

"You're certain?"

"I am."

As they closed the door behind them, Brendan looked at

his watch. Ten thirty. The news would be on in a minute. Perhaps it would mention the lads. He reached and turned the knob of the wireless.

The newscast had already begun, and the usual litany unwound itself. The American Secretary of State was in Brussels speaking to the members of the Common Market. The Israelis had executed nine terrorists captured during the bombing of a kibbutz near Jerusalem the month before. The President of the United States was reported to be mending after a water-ski mishap in Florida.

And now the national news. The voice changed to that of the down-country reporter. Gardai had arrested several young men believed to be associated with a car-theft ring in County Westmeath. They were being held in Mullingar. Rare Treasure, the Irish champion, had broken a leg while on a morning run. The famed stallion had been shot that evening. The G.A.A., financially affected by the recent drop in enthusiasm among the young, anticipated an all-out drive to gain membership.

And sports on the local level . . .

Brendan rubbed his face with his hands. What had gone wrong? Was the whole bloody thing a mirage? He pinched his flesh, like a child, to assure himself of reality.

The Special Bulletin signal startled him. He pressed close to the wireless. This was surely it. The voice droned:

We interrupt this broadcast to bring you a
special bulletin from Limerick. A young I.R.A. man was
found shot to death this evening in the area of
Canal Bank. The Gardai believe that death was caused
by suicide. The man was reputed to be
despondent following the arrest of several of his
companions in the wake of the recent attack on the
Minister for Justice, Mr. Patrick D. Mulcahy.
The dead man's name was Mr. Liam Daly. We will
bring you further details as they are received
from our correspondent, Mr. Michael Keough, in Limerick. And now back to the Irish Hospitals'
Sweepstake Programme for your entertainment . . .

The slow sleepy music followed. A crooner's voice joined in:

> You can wish upon a star,
> Makes no difference who you are.
> Anything your heart desires
> Will come to you.

Brendan brought his fist down on the cheap radio, knocking it from its stand above the table. However, it would not be shut up. It blared:

> Look for the silver lining,
> And it's the right thing for you to do.
> So won't you look . . .

He tore the cord from the socket. The kitchen fell into silence.

Chapter 15

Oliver Plunkett Street faced west. It was unprotected against the remnants of the Atlantic cloud banks that hurled themselves across the Clare Hills and down into this open area so often called "The Field." Brendan parked his Morris Minor at the curb and walked in the direction of the Daly home.

It seemed peculiar to him that the house was in near darkness. He had expected a grand wake in the old tradition, as the Daly family was well known and respected. And there were few cars parked outside and even fewer bicycles. It was a puzzle.

He shook the rain from his hat and pushed open the hall door. He heard a few muffled voices from the back of the house. He was about to search them out when the glow of candles from the front room caught his attention.

He stood in the doorway. The space before him danced in the light of the tapers like some unreal place where substance is an illusion and the perimeters must be remembered if one is not to suffer hallucination and suddenly stumble headlong into every altered object. But he knew the small room, the dresser, the grate, the mantel, the pictures on the wall. Hadn't he and Liam plotted together here with nothing but the fireglow as their light? Hadn't Liam's mother stuffed him with rashers and sausages, many a time here, so that he might not run off the road on his way home and be arrested for having drink taken? And he knew well the bandaged face of his friend who lay in death on the white sheets.

He sank to his knees and said aloud:

> Eternal rest grant unto him, O Lord,
> And may perpetual light shine upon him.
> May he rest in peace.

He reached out and touched the cold flesh. "God rest you," he said, his own body shaking and the tears flowing shamelessly down his face. "And may He love you always."

He drew himself up off his knees and walked quickly down the corridor towards the kitchen.

As he came into the light, he was surprised to find no one of his own in attendance. Granted, the men from the parish were in William Street Barracks, but what of all the others throughout the city and the far-lying townships? Had they forgotten that this was the death of a hero, a lad who twenty-four hours before had stood with him on the hill above Annacotty, had pointed to Mulcahy's Mercedes?

The few women present immediately left the room, having laid eyes on him. An old man who sat huddled in the corner, picked up his stick, gulped down the dregs of the Guinness in his glass, and went out through the scullery door. Only

Mrs. Daly remained in the tall chair by the fireplace.

He walked to her place and got down on his knees beside her. "Jesus, mam," he said, "when I heard, I couldn't believe my ears."

The woman remained silent, her face averted from his view. He squeezed her hand tightly. "It wasn't last night but I was saying to him . . ."

He was not prepared for what happened next. Instead of accepting his condolences, she quickly turned upon him. He felt her spittle on his cheek. Her face was contorted in a scowl. Her lips covered her teeth, like the lips of a snake drawn back over its fangs. "Curse you, you scum!" she cried. "You who made this house your own and then murdered . . ."

"Mrs. Daly. Oh, please, Mrs. Daly, will you hold your tongue. You don't know what you're saying," he begged of the woman who had often called herself his second mother. "Please stop . . ."

"I won't . . ."

"Mam, I wouldn't harm a hair on his head."

"You were the last one he was with."

"Mrs. Daly, I haven't seen him since yesterday night."

"Liar. He went out to your house before dark. Four or five o'clock. Said he, 'I'm off out to see Brendie. I won't have any supper.' And he tied his red scarf about his neck and went off as happy as Larry. Next thing, the misfortune, he's coming in the door a corpse, in the arms of two Guards, a hole in his lovely head the size of a half crown."

"O my Jesus."

"You! You!"

"No! No!"

In his stupor, he began shaking the slight frame of the woman. She cried out in fear of him, and her terror returned her sanity. "All right. All right, Brendan. But let go of me," she said. "Please let go of me."

He fell to the floor. "I'm sorry," he said over and over.

Mrs. Daly's face changed. She looked down at him. "Maybe you didn't kill him, Brendie," she said, "but you brought him into the movement. And one of them killed him."

"But the radio said suic——"

"The farthest thing from my boy's mind was doing away with himself. He couldn't have been happier when he left here tonight. He was all excited about something that yourself and himself had done. Proud. No. Don't tell me suicide. Murder is what it is."

"But who?"

"One of your own. Surely it wasn't an Orangeman come down from the North to pick on an innocent boy . . ."

"But, Mrs. Daly, it couldn't have been one of ours. We're not animals that we turn on ourselves. If he had an enemy, then I'd have had an enemy. It doesn't make sense."

"Does it make sense to you that not a soul who called him friend is under this roof except yourself?"

"A lot of them are in jail. Liam was the only one from the parish who wasn't arrested besides myself."

"Maybe you're free, Brendan Donnelly, because you sold him out to . . ." She was working herself up into a convulsion again.

He grasped her face, but still her voice screamed, "And he won't have a friend but myself to pray over him tomorrow when they lower him into the ground. Not a friend. I've seen it before. He did something to displease them. So they murdered him and will allow him to be buried in shame as the final punishment."

"Mrs. Daly," Brendan said, "calm yourself. Don't be getting upset, now. I'll guarantee you that Liam's funeral will be black with crowds of our own. And I guarantee you, too, that I'll go right to the top for answers on this awful thing. If someone did it, I'll take his fucking life myself . . ."

He wheeled off the floor and kissed the old woman on the forehead.

"Brendie, don't!" she said. But he was gone out through the curtains and into the hallway.

Chapter 16

B efore Buckley could anchor the hall door of his house, Brendan Donnelly was through the porchway and into the kitchen of the dark little Corporation cottage. "Now, Raef," he said, "I want the fucking truth out of you, or by God I'll beat you within an inch of your life."

"Brendan. Brendan. Do you want the Peelers in on top of us? Stop. Stop. I'll talk to you if you'll be civil."

"Spit it out!"

"I will. I will. Give me me breath."

The clerk straightened his collar, looked about him cautiously, and leaned forward. "Brendie," he said, "I don't know much more than yourself."

"What *do* you know?"

"Only what I've heard through the ranks."

"And that is?"

"That Liam Daly, God rest him, did away with himself. I swear to you, I don't know anything else. None of the lads do neither. Even the Guards are certain that it was suicide, from what I hear."

"Where did he get the gun?"

"Who knows? You can buy those old war souvenirs at any pawn shop. Even Nestor's carry a few of them now and again."

"What does Riordan have to say about all of this?"

"He knows nothing."

"He said that?"

"His man did."

"What else was put out?"

"That we were to stay away from the wake. The place was being watched by Guards all around the clock."

"Why wasn't *I* told that?"

"No one could get ahold of you. We sent a man out, but your house was in darkness and your car was gone. We guessed as much that you went to Daly's."

"I did."

"I don't think that the Guards will put a seem in it, though. You and Liam were good old pals."

Brendan rested against the table. "I don't understand this at all, Raef," he said. "It's beyond me."

"The funeral? Will you be going?"

"Are you taking leave of your senses, man? Of course I'm going."

"But Brendie . . ."

"No buts. He was one of us. And since when did friendship come after bloody politics? Politics don't mean jack shit if we're not all for one and one for all. Do they?"

"I suppose not."

"I'll see all of you there."

"Right. But Riordan might not . . ."

"Fuck Riordan!"

Brendan turned on his heel. He had not taken two steps when Buckley called in a low voice, "Brendie!"

"What?"

"Something else."

"Out with it."

"There's no one behind bars, now. They let them out this morning at the crack of dawn. They couldn't hold them."

Chapter 17

Brendan Donnelly knelt in the darkness of the confessional. He shifted his weight so as to relieve the pain he felt in his shins. He cursed the knots in the wood beneath them, but reminded himself that this was a place of punishment and not comfort.

In the blackness, he heard the voice of an old woman as she rattled off her sins, sometimes repeating the same transgressions over and over. The priest's murmur was as exasperating. Why didn't he tell her that she was blameless, that her soul was as white as the day she made her First Communion? He hated Sunday morning Confessions. The pews were invariably filled with only the very young and the very old. He should have gone last night after leaving the Daly house instead of drowning his sorrows in a feed of porter. His head ached now from the effects and from the bombardment of trifles coming from out of the gloom:

Father, I read my neighbor . . .
Father, I didn't come into Mass until
after the First Gospel . . .
Father, I forgot to pray for my mother's rest . . .
Father, I spoke about my neighbor behind her back . . .

Jesus! That he might have her sins in place of the weight that hung on his shoulders. The bandaged face of Liam appeared before his eyes. He saw, too, the sorrowing features of old Mrs. Daly. The muscles in his chest tightened. He tried to arrange the words that would suit the full explication of his sin. He must not omit one iota for fear that another sin might be earned into the bargain.

Suddenly, the prattle stopped. He heard the creaking of the boards as the woman raised herself. The door opening and closing. The next penitent entering. The voice of the priest whispering an aspiration to himself. And then the slide easing back. The face of the confessor was silhouetted in the half-light.

"Bless me, Father, for I have sinned. It has been almost a year since my last Confession. In that time, I committed the following sins against my Most Loving Master . . ." Brendan said.

And not unlike the old woman, he accused himself of all the minor transgressions memorized since childhood. Profanity. Disobedience to his mother. Anger at his brother and sister. Occasional immodest thoughts. Pride.

After a short pause to catch his wind, he said, "Father, I was the cause of a man's death."

He expected the priest to come through the mesh, but the cleric merely asked in a slow whisper, "Did you take his life with your own hand?"

"Oh, no, Father. He was with me in the movement. They found his body last night. Suicide, they say."

The priest stirred and seemed to be smoothing out his cassock. "Why then," he asked, "do you accuse yourself?"

"Because, Father, I brought him into the movement. It is somehow because of that membership that he is dead. I bear the brunt of the guilt for his death."

The priest put his hand to his mouth. "Nonsense," he said. "You're creating a storm in a teacup. There was no conscious intention of taking this man's life at the time that you introduced him to the movement."

"No, but . . ."

"Well, there you are. You committed no sin. You're proud of your membership in the movement, as any man should be who stands on the side of justice and . . ."

"Yes."

"So you are safe from mortal sin. A small venial sin may have taken place. Nothing to worry about."

"But, Father, in my heart I know that I am responsible . . ."

"My son," the priest said with laughter in his voice, "our sins are made in the rational mind. It is there that we accept or reject God. Conscious rejection of God is a rare thing. As a result, few people commit mortal sin. You never intended to isolate yourself from God when you brought this man into the movement, did you?"

Brendan was silent. The priest continued to explain the Church's new standing on the matter of sin. But his words went unheeded. Brendan was concentrating on the face which now appeared more distinct to him in the shadows. A boyish face. Not more than twenty-five. Just out of the seminary. Lecturing with confidence and authority. *Ex cathedra*. His arse!

Brendan left his knees. The priest stopped. "The Confession is not over yet, my son," he said.

"Ah, but it is, Father," Brendan answered. "You're out of

your bloody mind. Go and tell your fancy theories to the dead boy down in 'The Field.' A deal of good words like yours will do *him.*"

The confessional door slammed behind him with such force that many in the congregation of the church turned their heads from the altar where the Consecration was taking place. But Brendan did not acknowledge their dismay. He broke through the exit at the rear and ran down the granite steps and into the sunlight.

He was tired of walking the street and decided to distract his mind from the experience by stopping off to have a pint at Laffey's. He had missed Mass through his anger, and this, too, was of no consolation to him.

When the bartender brought his Guinness, Brendan said, "Lord God, but aren't the times changing. A man wouldn't know where he was, some days."

"You're right. It's not the same country we knew, Brendie. And religion is powerless to change it—and doesn't *want* to, by all accounts. That's why I don't go anymore . . ."

"You're right. Fucking hippies in the pews looking up at those in the pulpit."

"You hit the nail on the head."

Brendan's face brightened. He had meant to circle the subject, but now in no time he was in the thick of it. "Would you believe it," he said, "that I tried to go to Confession this very day and was told that I had no sins to tell. That most of the world is walking around innocent, as innocent as the driven snow. 'There's no such thing as mortal sins anymore,' says your man. Can you beat that?"

"God be with long ago. Father Creed up in St. John's would ate you out of the box for just swearing."

"Those were the days when they gave you a mile for your half dollar."

"Right."

Brendan leaned forward on the bar. "There's no more of them left, I suppose?" he said.

Farrell, the bartender, looked up from the glass that he was drying. "Well," he said, "most of them are dead and gone. But there's one . . ."

Brendan tried desperately to contain his excitement. "There is?" he said.

"Yes. My missus was talking about some priest that scandalized her over nothing, a while back. Father Griffin, I think, was his name. In fact, I'm almost certain."

"Go on! Here in the city?"

"Right. St. Michael's. Or St. Joseph's. Or maybe St. Munchin's. That's the part that I'm not certain of. But she was ashamed of her life coming out of the box."

Brendan finished his pint and excused himself to the jakes. But once out in the backyard, he pressed his hat down on his head and scaled the low stile that led to Anne Street. From there it was only a five minute walk to St. Michael's.

The church in Denmark Street faced south. Brendan had rarely ventured inside its doors as he had always regarded it as a cubbyhole. It seemed awkward, out of place there on the corner, without a lawn or a gate or a decent bit of shrubbery to give it character. It was a city parish, which meant that it enjoyed little prestige among the other more residential ones. Where would it gain identity? From the City Market? The Guards' Barracks at William Street? The fish stores on O'Connell Avenue? The travel agencies on Sarsfield Street? No. It was a dull place.

Mass was long ended when he arrived. A few remaining women turned to look at him as he entered, but, their mouths still quivering in prayer, they returned to their various near-trances before the Stations of the Cross. He looked up and down the aisles. Only one confessional light burned in the unnatural blackness. He walked in its direction.

He could hear the priest recite his Holy Office behind the curtain. Perhaps this was he. The young ones never had a prayerbook in their hands. But he had to be certain. He looked up at the name. Father Dannagher. Nothing like Griffin. He turned away in disappointment.

But what of the unlighted boxes? He'd try each one. If he found Father Griffin's name, he'd go to the sacristy and ask for private Confession.

Quickly he crossed the aisle and walked to the first box near the altar. Father Nagle. He genuflected to the Altar of Repose and stepped backwards.

The next cubicle was that of Father Reagan. And the following one was unnamed, used only for visiting priests or retreat masters. That left only one to the rear of the church. He said a short aspiration to St. Anthony, the patron of finding, and faced the shafts of light that penetrated the shadows at the back.

But his search was useless. Father Cavanaugh, the box read. He drew a deep breath and put his hand to his face. What was he going to do? He could not face Liam Daly's funeral tomorrow with such a mark on his soul. It would be unnatural. And a mockery.

Just then a voice behind him said, "What are you looking for, sir? Might I help you?"

Brendan swung about to face the sacristan. "Looking for?" he said.

"Yes. You seemed to be confused . . ."

"Oh. I was searching for Father Griffin. I don't see his name."

"Father Griffin. He's been gone this many a month. They moved him to St. Joseph's uptown. Now whether he's still there or not, it's hard to say. A terrible man. We lost half the parish over him . . ."

"You did, now?"

Brendan left the church. He'd use his car to get to St. Joseph's. There was little need in running his legs off.

But St. Joseph's was as unlucky for him as the last. No Father Griffin on the boxes and no real knowledge of his whereabouts on the part of the deacon. Parteen, the man had heard. But that was only the wisp of a thought in his head. It could be related to a different priest or a different matter entirely, he said. But then again, that association was better than nothing, though the country parish didn't seem to be the appropriate place for "the fireball," as the acolytes had christened Father Griffin.

Brendan departed with his thanks to the man. The drive across the Shannon into Parteen wouldn't do him any harm. And if he failed to find the Griffin priest, as he was partly certain would be the case, then he'd take the road east to Jack Walsh's in Blackwater for a few Baby Powers to calm his nerves.

In the church at Parteen, he made the usual touching of the Holy Water to his forehead and genuflected. He looked about. At the shrine to the Virgin stood a candelabrum with nearly all its penny lights extinguished. A red lamp burned before the altar to St. Joseph. The main altar was the least distinguished. It consisted of a square wooden table, topped by a crucifix, and situated in the center of a worn green carpet. There was no pulpit. A lopsided lectern took its place.

Something was missing. Of course—the confessionals! He gazed all about, but he could not locate a sign of the traditional box. Didn't they have sins in this part of the country? he thought as he edged towards the shabby altar. Was he in the right church? Sure he was—Protestants didn't believe in the Virgin.

It was then that he noticed the open doorway to the right of the altar. Someone was bound to be in the room beyond, he thought. The sacristan surely wouldn't leave the door open and risk the theft of chalices and other holy vessels and vestments. He'd cross the altar and try there.

When he reached the opening, he was startled by a voice from inside. "Hurry up! Hurry up!" it said. "I'm not going to sit here all day hearing Confessions. I haven't even had my breakfast yet. One o'clock Mass. Who ever heard of it in the city? 'Tradition,' the Bishop says. Tradition for a lot of country mugs and lazy city ones. Hurry up, and be quick about it."

Brendan looked into the room. A white-haired priest sat facing the wall. Behind him stood a prie-dieu with two ragged cushions. "Father Griffin?" he almost shouted. "Father Griffin?"

The priest arched his head. "Who do you think I am?" he said. "Get in here and be quick about it, I don't have all day."

Brendan rushed to the kneeler. He blessed himself and began the usual lead-in. "Bless me, Father, for I have sinned . . ."

The fear of his sin came upon him again, and it was mingled with the expectation of the reprimand and the penance which would follow. But it was a rightful terror. Fear of sin. Fear of its punishment. Union once again with God and man. It was almost pleasurable for him to hold back the final admission and circle it with a few venial offenses. Slowly he said, "I showed great anger . . ."

The priest's head leaned to one side. Brendan's voice wavered. He would skip the maneuvering. With bold enunciation he said, "I was the cause of a man losing his life. He took his own life, or others took it for him, because of circumstances made possible by me. I am seeped in his blood."

He waited. The outburst would come any second now. Brendan winced. Jesus have mercy on him. He already began his Act of Contrition in his head. He shivered in anticipation of the verbal flogging.

The loud and indecent sound seemed to be coming from the priest. Brendan looked about him, then turned his head so as to focus on the face of the confessor. He drew back suddenly. A smile was crossing the lips, revealing big discolored teeth and allowing the tongue to lie extended. The old man was snoring loudly.

Chapter 18

Colum had left the house late in the afternoon, saying that he would catch the night Mass at the Augustinians'. It had not been an ordinary Sunday. First of all, Brendan was nowhere to be found. His absence had upset the usual ritual. There was no way to Mass. As a result, Josie and her mother took the Corbally bus. Colum stayed in bed. The dinner of pig's head had to be abandoned and brawn sandwiches made to take its place. And Seoirse Hayes anchored his rear end by the fireplace in the early afternoon and gave a running commentary on the Limerick-Tipperary football game.

This was the first time that Colum had missed Mass since he and Tom Fagan, his close friend at the novitiate, had hitchhiked into Boyle to see an American film. Afterwards, they had to telephone their prefect to come and get them. Colum remembered the look on his face when they'd explained that only two cars had passed in three hours. "Gentlemen," he said in his girllike voice, "I'm not at all certain you'll make Brothers. I have a definite feeling that those who miss the celebration of Christ come alive in the Eucharist have poor place in religion. You regard your time at the monastery as a holiday, a respite from the hardships of life on the outside, and yet you are curious of the pleasures that exist beyond the walls. You can't have your cake and eat it. They are two different things. I will make a recommendation to the Master . . ."

"Sir," Colum interrupted, "I request that we be allowed to explain the circumstances to the Master of Novices. I believe that he may take a dim view of how you take *your* pleasure and the quality of *your* vocation."

"Get in," the prefect said. "Get in and be quick about it."

Of course, nothing more was heard of the incident. Colum had merely called his bluff. It was a cruel joke that the prefect often enjoyed the company of young boys in his rooms after lights out. There was not a shred of truth to the matter.

That had been almost three years ago. Colum wondered if Tom, now a Brother in the Seychelles Islands, ever remembered the episode, ever relished it as he himself did.

He reached the George. The excitement of the moment made his hand tremble on the handle of the door. If Rayana still had her car, they might drive to the Green Hills or take the road north to Driscoll's. The come-all-ye songs of the latter place might interest her sense of what was "Irish."

The vestibule was crowded. Foreigners anxious about the transport of their luggage to the waiting Shannon Airport limousine. Natives on holiday, not at all certain if their patience would last until every multicolored tourist was out of the country. He edged towards the desk and faced the same receptionist from before. "Good evening," Colum said.

"Evening, sir."

"Would you please ring Miss Duggan's room for me?"

"Duggan?"

"Yes."

"Now that strikes a bell. Where? Where? Oh, yes. The American woman."

"Right," Colum's voice betrayed his exasperation.

"Ah, lad, but she's gone off. Left around noon."

Colum caught his breath. The old man seemed to be enjoying the situation, a pay-back for all the disparagement suffered at the hands of youth. But then, as though satisfied with having inflicted enough punishment, the man said, "But, sir, the woman left a message for you. I have it here. She asked me to hand it to you."

Colum took the pink envelope. He reached in his pocket and found a shilling piece. "Here," he said.

The old porter smiled. "No," he said, "she took good care of me. There's no need."

"Take it anyway."

"No. It's enough of us that are taking more than our share."

Colum left by the side door. The night was still bright. As he walked, he tore open the envelope. The message read:

I mentioned my "old man" to you. Well, he was
passing through Limerick and paid me a visit—someone
at home must have given him my itinerary. He
wants me to go and see relatives of his in Kerry. So far
as they know, we're still living in marital bliss.
We've been separated for over three years. Of course,
being Irish, we must keep up the face at all
costs. Right?

Drop by at the end of the week. I'll be looking for you.

Love,
Rayana

What an idiot he had been to have not caught on. Yet he could not accuse her of lying, in the true sense of that word. All at once, he wished that he could scream out at the top of his voice. He had gotten more than he'd bargained for, and the realization frightened him. It was one thing to have talk of his meeting with a strange girl, but quite another if that girl were married. He could not afford this sort of thing. His family. His job. He thanked God that it hadn't gone farther. Surely nobody had seen him in the car the night before? And the porter had called Rayana "Miss" not more than two minutes before. The smug old man knew nothing. He had merely looked confident because Colum had been temporarily replaced by another man. Somehow, he felt that Rayana's husband was older than he, closer to the hotel servant's age. He examined each detail again. It was airtight. He was perfectly safe.

There would be other Rayanas but in another place. He must start going to Dublin or Galway or Cork on weekends. He'd have no bother buying an old jalopy on the hire-purchase. If Brendan, who was unemployed, could drive about the country, then, by, God, so could he.

At Poor Man's Kilkee, he stopped to watch the sun set. It

showed a golden face to the city as it momentarily released itself from the roof of clouds above it and was drawn almost immediately into the mouth of the river. He felt nothing for Rayana. He had formulated a solution to his previous attraction. Instead of seeing her in the light of her perfume, hair, teeth, and smile, so mysterious and enticing to him up to an hour ago, he chose now to visualize her through the eyes of her husband. He reasoned that familiarity must of necessity diminish sensuousness, destroy spontaneity. That man would know every crevice of her body, every imperfection, every unsightly secretion. With this as his base, it was easy for Colum to declare her as used, owned, no longer fresh, no more a tantalizing idea, but instead a drab reality.

The thoughts of school invaded his mind as they always did on Sunday evenings. If only the Monday morning classroom—all classrooms—could be erased forever.

Chapter 19

It was late on Sunday night when Brendan Donnelly pulled up to the Park railway gates. They were closed against him. Bloody excursions, he thought. He waited until the train passed. It was then that he noticed the hunched figure near the stile. Perhaps old Davy Shanny waiting for the smell of the Guinness to subside before returning to the hearth of sisters and mother. He lowered the window. "Is that you, Davy?" he said. "Can I give you a lift up to the house?"

The face that turned to look at him was not that of Davy but of his own brother. "Colum!" he said. "Someone will think you're a bogey man there in the dark. Get in. Get in."

They were at the Bonard Corner before Brendan spoke again. "I suppose you heard of the tragedy?" he said.

"What tragedy? The shooting of the Israeli hostages in Libya?"

"Fuck, no! Liam's death."

"Liam? Liam Daly?"

"You didn't hear?"

"No."

"What is this bloody place coming to!"

They had reached their own yard. The house was in darkness. Brendan turned off the engine. He pressed forward on the steering wheel. "Christ, Colum," he said, "I don't know what to make of it. It's giving me the creeps."

"How did it happen?"

"He was shot to death."

"Go on!"

"No. Last night on the Canal Bank. The Guards say suicide. His mother won't have that. She says that he was as happy as Larry on his way out to see me. And Riordan's man says that none of our crowd had a thing to do with it."

"Do you have any suspicions?"

"Not a one."

"Would he be capable of suicide, do you think?"

"Ah, no. He was a bit shaky that morning before we hit Mulcahy, but so were we all. It's the price of the game."

"He wasn't the most sound, you know?"

"What do you mean? What do you know about him?"

"I went to school with him."

"And? What does that prove?"

"He quit after his Intermediate."

"So? I never got that far, myself."

"He quit because of a nervous breakdown. He spent almost a year in the Mental Home."

"Oh, save us. I never knew!"

Colum reached over and touched his brother. "Come on. Let's go in the house," he said. "I'll put on a pot of tea for us."

"Thanks."

Once inside the house, Colum busied himself at the electric cooker. "By the way," he asked, "what time is the funeral?"

"Eleven in the morning."

"Would you mind if I went along with you?"

"But what about school?"

"To hell with it. I'll call in."

"You're welcome to come along."

"I'd like that."

Something between them had come alive, though Colum could not name it. Perhaps it was his own letdown that evening which, coupled with Brendan's grief, drew them together. Or, then, maybe it was the insignificancy of his own distress, as faced with the magnitude of murder, which took him forward into the circle and entrapped him in the dance that he had only recently come to know. But what if it went deeper in the blood? To examine it further would be to destroy its force. He chose to leave it to its own energy. "The tea is almost ready," he said.

"I'm famished," Brendan answered. "I can use it."

Chapter 20

The funeral of Liam Daly was a success, when one thought of it in the light of the six hundred mourners, who included about ninety men from the movement, all decked out in their black berets and carrying between them the tricolor of the Republic, which they laid reverently across the bier. However, the honor guard was not permitted by Mrs. Daly, a detail that unsettled Brendan but went unnoticed by his brother. In its place, four Franciscans, a Redemptorist, and a Dominican led the cortege. And there were mothers, too, and children within them. And prams with babies asleep under their hoods, and mongrel dogs of every dimension tagging alongside. It was a funeral that touched the heart, as those of the young always do, spreading out before it a wave of sorrow and absurdity, which could only be daunted by the great surge of union that tragedy brings in its wake. This was a funeral of the Old City, of King's Island, the parish. Those who came out of alleyways and churches, and stood standing on the footpaths, felt somehow alien and remote and wished for belonging in this gaudy tide.

Colum marched with his brother at the edge of the crowd. He had not been able to conjure up the feelings that he had experienced at the passing of the other funeral cortege, a few days before. His impotency annoyed him, and he diverted his thoughts.

The hearse stopped at the traffic lights. He heard two men chat on the curb. "God help us," one said. "What makes them go into the movement at all?"

"What makes an animal that lives in a hole search after the sunlight?" his companion answered. "Sure this fucking country has nothing to offer the young lads growing up. What can they do? Work for the likes of the Corporation and spend their lives shoveling shit? Or get an education and spend the time looking out the window of an office at the same shit? Will you stop! Every man, woman, and child deserves a few minutes of fame and fortune and excitement. The movement provides that. More power to the rebels, I says. If I was a lad again, I'd join up tomorrow."

"And be a corpse like this poor misfortune the next day."

"You don't know what you're talking about. And if I did catch a bullet, wouldn't I be a hero, a man apart from all the sheep . . ."

"And dead into the bargain."

As the funeral passed the Christian Brothers' School at Sexton Street, Colum regained some of his confidence. He looked out from the crowd of parishmen at the alien place and cursed it, and wished that he might never return to it. Yet he knew that he was capable of functioning within its dark granite walls and, at the same time, within the arms and feet and mouths and eyes of all those about him. The mental construct gave him a sense of duality that exhilarated him.

After the graveside prayers, Mrs. Daly, in the company of many older women, came towards them. She put out her hand to Brendan. "Thank you, love," she said. "I'll never be able to repay you. And about Saturday night, I was troubled . . ."

"Forget it," Brendan said. "It never happened."

"All right," she said, "but don't be a stranger to our house. The door is always wide open to you."

"I know."

She turned to Colum, and to his surprise, put her hand to his face. "You're Alfie's youngest, aren't you?" she said. "You have his eyes. He was the smart one. But a lovely man. You come from good stock. God bless you." With that, she faced into the crowds and left them.

Colum had been taken aback by her words. Their accuracy had drawn up for him again the image of his father's face. The eyes. How well he remembered them. Eyes that knew the response, long before it was made; knew the excuse, long before its falsehood pricked the conscience. He scraped the clay beneath him with his shoe.

When Mrs. Daly had gone, Brendan said, "Look over there beyond the headstones."

Colum looked. A black limousine stood parked under the trees, its front windows rolled halfway down, the rear section curtained off from view. "Who is it?" he asked.

"Probably Riordan or some other bigwig. I'm surprised that they showed their faces."

At that moment, they saw a hand reach from the front window. It waved. They heard a man's voice call out, "Donnelly. Donnelly."

Brendan responded by pointing to himself and his brother, but the hand shook vigorously and then pointed at him alone. The order was clear.

"I'll be back in a minute," Brendan said. "Wait for me across the street at the Fair Tavern."

Colum watched him pick his way across the untidy stretch of grass and stones. When he reached the car, he removed his hat and stood like a schoolboy awaiting the sentence of the headmaster. Eventually, he stooped and entered. Colum pitied his brother. How easily he could be manipulated and molded. Colum felt a resentment for Riordan rise inside himself. Was it a consequence of the man's ability to place his brother in a position of servitude? Or did it run to other things? For all the talk of admiration, why hadn't *he* been called to the car, too? Of course, it may not have been Riordan at all but one of his subordinates.

As he crossed the macadam path that led from the Daly grave, his mind rested again on the terrible eyes of his father. Yet for all of his anger and power, Colum remembered, he had never actually beaten any of his children, though once or twice he had come close. Isolation from his good graces and the magnificent flurry of life which surrounded him had been punishment enough.

Riordan sat across the seat from Brendan. He removed his leather gloves as he said, "Brendan, how nice to see you again, so soon."

Brendan did not answer. He fidgeted with the hat in his hands. He had guessed that the words with Buckley would draw fire. But he was prepared to take the consequences now.

He was surprised when Riordan said instead, "A powerful funeral, though it's unfortunate that he should have gone the way he did. But, in a way, he gave his life for the rest of us."

Brendan's head cocked to the side. "How do you mean, sir?" he asked.

"Well, he knew that he wouldn't hold up if the Guards got him. So I can only assume . . ."

"His mother will have nothing to do with that story."

"Lord knows, if only we were as our mothers see us to be."

"I can't believe that he'd go that far, really. I mean, I worked with him. He wasn't made of ice—none of us are. But he was solid enough, a little nervous at times, maybe . . ."

"He'd had a breakdown, once. Did you know that?"

"I did. My brother mentioned it."

"He did?"

"Yes. He said that it happened when Liam was at Sexton Street."

"It was a few years ago. It's been reported to me that after your little caper the other day, he was very shaky. There was a bit of an incident in a pub on Sandmall. He stormed out of there, after shouting that they'd all be surprised if they knew that Mulcahy's assailant had relatives in the parish."

"Go on! He didn't!"

"Yes, he did." Riordan's voice had lost its conversational tone and was now austere. "And so, Brendan," he continued, "my words to you the other day were very pertinent. We want no more novices in the movement. We're professionals, not scallywags. In future, do all jobs alone or with tried men. No more novices. That's final. And further, this matter of Daly's death is to be left closed. The Guards say suicide. Suicide it is. No one within our group harmed him. There is no possibility that the other side had a thing to do with it, either. Any nosing about may place the organization in jeopardy. Is that clear?"

"Yes." Brendan's head was bowed as he replied.

"And now I must be off."

Brendan put his hand on the door lever and turned it. The cold air rushed into the cramped space and threw his hair back from his eyes.

The door slammed shut, and he was left on the pavement. The limousine eased into the diminishing crowd. It turned on the center driveway, angled west, and left by the side gate. Some girls on bicycles passed him, their miniskirts revealing their young legs. He closed his eyes against the onslaught.

He would not go to the Munster Fair Tavern. Colum would understand; he was not a child. Brendan knew that he must face the burden of his thoughts alone. My God, my God, where had all the old feeling gone? Where was the pride that had dazzled his father's face on an Easter Sunday morning as he marched in the crowd of old patriots? As he held Brendan's hand in the pub afterwards and spoke of the Rising of 1916? As the elder Donnelly touched his comrades, then bent with age but alive in spirit, and talked of the selfless surrender of all that was precious, so that men might not be animals but walk with decency under the sun? His belly tightened, not so much at Riordan's slight reprimand, but at his neglect, neglect at the issue of one man's loss of life. So it was unfortunate that Liam Daly had died, but lucky that it had all been so convenient, so tidy? Had it been this way when he'd joined, just a year or so back? he asked himself. He recalled the night that Declan Purcell had touched his shoulder in Miss Luby's bar in Athlunkard Street. It had been a miserable week of rain and mud. (A week, too, of turndowns on jobs.) The locals were huddled together by the fire. Suddenly, the night's programme on RTE was interrupted by the news of an I.R.A. rescue at Mountjoy Jail. The boyos had landed a helicopter and lifted their man right out of the prison yard.

The pub was thrown into an uproar. "Jesus!" one man said. "Just like Our Lord's Ascension into Heaven!"

"Geniuses!" another shouted. "There's been nothing like them!"

"Nor ever will be. A different breed entirely."

"They could be forgiven anything, no matter how vexed you'd get at them."

"True patriots."

"Warriors of the Red Branch," a small man with a wart exclaimed.

"Was anyone killed?"

"No. Just two fucking louts of Guards shot through the arse."

"Full power to the I.R.A."

"Fuck all foreigners and strangers."

He had felt the weight on his shoulder. "You could be one of us," Purcell's voice whispered. "Just as your father was, in his day. We could use you. The pay would be . . ."

"I wouldn't join for the money."

"I understand. But doesn't the army of a country pay its men? And we're the only true army of the South. We pay decent . . ."

"Where would I go to join?"

Purcell slipped him a white card. "See you at the next meeting," he said. "I'll vouch for you myself."

"Thanks."

He saw the boyo edge through the crowd and leave by the rear door of the pub. He felt all at once proud and powerful and part of something great though frightening, as he gazed at the confusion on the television screen. Guards and soldiers everywhere. Amadans about their amadans' work. He was bitter about being idle, ashamed of it. He remembered the writing on his last pink slip:

> Intelligent fellow. Has a lot of energy. Has to
> work at his own pace. But he lacks the most basic
> standard of education for any advancement with
> this company . . .

He spat into the sawdust. He'd show all these midgets with their uniforms and outfits. Their letters of recommendation and education tucked into their arse pockets—and nothing in their heads. They'd be the ones to look when he passed, from this day forward.

His thoughts came back to the present. He was sure that the movement hadn't changed. It was Riordan. It was his foreign nature that spread out this breath of ice before it. Yes. That was it.

He crossed Blackboy Road. He looked about for a familiar face after the ritual. But there was none. Few waited around anymore after a burial.

Chapter 21

B rendan was not present at the supper table. But Colum
made excuses for him when his mother and Josie
inquired. "Ah," he said, "he had to see a man after the
funeral. He'll be back in a while. He won't leave himself
hungry."

The meal continued in silence, until Josie said, "What's
this we hear about you and some American dolly uptown?"

For a second, the mention of Rayana caught him unawares.
Had someone spotted him that night? Was the word out all
over town? He pretended not to have heard. He turned the
page of the *Limerick Leader.* One of the Third World leaders
was complaining of an invasion of his country's borders. As
usual, the United Nations was hedging.

Josie continued her harangue. "Out driving in the country.
Dancing at the George. There's no knowing to the likes of
the swanky stuff young men are up to today. Oh, the
blessings of education . . ."

"Be quiet and eat your supper," the mother said. "Leave
him alone. He has the right to do as he pleases. No one
criticizes yourself and Seoirse, out there under the street light
until all hours. Children these days . . ."

Colum laughed nervously. "There," he said. "Mam's told
you—sex maniac!"

"Now, don't you be going on either," the mother said.
"I'm not for either one of you. There was never a word of
scandal about your father and myself. We saved our
romancing until the fit time—*after* we were married. I hope
that the two of you keep the same in mind. As for your
brother, Lord knows what he do be up to! But at least where
he goes nobody talks. They're men's places, and nothing
ever passes their doors."

The mother's words surprised her two children. Colum
made a long face to Josie when the old woman left the table

and went to her room to prepare for evening devotions at St. Patrick's. Josie returned the expression.

"Seriously, though, Colum," Josie said, "what happened between yourself and Ellen is no business of mine, but the poor kid is taking it very hard. And then this talk about your American friend."

"Rayana."

"Jesus, Mary, and Joseph! What kind of an unnatural name is that for anyone?"

"What are they saying?"

"That you were seen driving. Kissing on the street . . ."

"Nothing else?" The words slipped out of his mouth. He knew his error immediately and tried to correct it. "I mean . . ."

Josie had caught his ploy. "Colum," she said, "oh, Colum, I hope you did nothing shameful. If Mam or Dad . . ."

"Jesus, Josie! Dad? He's dead and buried. And Mam . . ." But he knew that it was useless. His life was so desperately removed from hers. He felt momentarily ashamed of the separation. But his mind suggested to him that it was her plight if all that she cared for was marriage to lazy Seoirse, a clique of fat children hanging out of her breasts, and drudgery from daylight until dark—all held together by the guiding star of outdated morality and ritual. Oh, the poor fool! He saw her eyes and mouth as though they were affixed to the face of a stranger. Nonetheless, he tried to shatter the realization by reaching out and putting his fingers in hers. But his action was not spontaneous, and he knew it well. "Listen," he said, "I did nothing for which I might be ashamed, if that's what you're worried about. Now, will you stop going on about Reverend Mother Ellen Sullivan."

"Ah, come on now, Colum. This isn't like you. We're not hardhearted people. It'd be reasonable to give one of the snooty bitches uptown the slip, but Ellen is just a little girl out of secondary school. She cares about you, Colum. The sun shines out of you, so far as she's concerned. She doesn't deserve to be hurt. And she's family into the bargain; that makes it even worse."

He had forgotten that Ellen was a distant
with his father's people in some involve
remembered very clearly the old man's c
that has to be fought without, but leave
your own. If you don't, you're no better t
How simplistic a view, he thought. But perhaps it was
viable one in the day of his father, when the world was
perceived as manageable. "Okay, okay," he said. "I get the
point. I'll give her a call one of these nights. Maybe after I'm
through with exams and have an ounce of time to myself."

"It wouldn't hurt you, Colum."

He was annoyed with himself that he could not conjure up
exactly the full features of Ellen. And it had only been four
days! He could see her dark brown hair. Her lips. Her eyes.
But not all of these at once. Still, he had to admit, the
mention of her brought a nostalgia. He thought of Ellen's
peasant purity matched with Rayana's world-weariness. He
looked at his sister. She, for all of her off-color remarks, was
clad in the same chastity as Ellen. It was everywhere you
looked in the parish. His separation from it gave him a lonely
feeling, so much like the unsettling images one relishes of
disastrous summers spent away from home, at some remote
resort, but which glow in the memory for all the years
between. But this suggestion, too, reminded him of the
freedom and individuality and isolation that he had lately
come to cherish.

Chapter 22

In the first week in June, St. Michael's Christian Brothers'
Secondary School closed for the summer. It was an
occasion of excitement to Colum. He imagined the long
days stretching ahead, free of the shadow of the impending
September that would surely come but which now could be
relegated to a far-off eternity. And, also, much to his surprise

and delight, he was paid for the holiday. It was decent of the Superior, Brother Roland, to do that, he thought, especially when he had only worked at the school for the few remaining months of the spring.

At first, he occupied his holidays with early swims at Plassey, followed by the long run back home to face a breakfast of rashers and eggs and black Matterson's pudding and the coddling attention of his mother. She had him all to herself now, she said. It reminded her of years gone by when she had taken him everywhere and anywhere. How they used to sit by the fire in the morning then, like two old crones, hashing over their plans for the day's shopping. And Colum didn't mind his mother's rhapsodies. He had always been close to her, principally because she had afforded him a certainty of mood and endearment which his father had never provided. It was impossible to gauge his father's tempers. It seemed that Brendan was their only arbiter.

Though Colum had contributed most of his pay packet towards the running of the house, a habit he had practiced since his days as a bar boy at Driscoll's pub in Corbally, he still retained a sufficient amount to act as a down payment on a small car. However, as the idyllic days drifted by with so much contentment and ease, he forgot temporarily about the car. He forgot, too, about Rayana and Ellen and the momentary agitation which they had introduced into his life. Not that he forgot the impressions that the experience of them had afforded him. Oh, no. In the quiet of each afternoon, as he sat in front of his typewriter, he recalled every detail and implication of his reaction to the two girls, especially Rayana. He examined each one under lights which its reality had never enjoyed. With the introduction of "what if," he transcribed, changed, festered, ballooned the example into the delicate half-truth of his fiction. As a result, his stories left their original dimension of wood and rock and water and took on the cloak of intensity and disconsolation.

Towards the middle of June, the National Grants for Young Writers were awarded. A man from Galway (a student at the University) won the novel category. The poetry prize went to a Waterford girl, a clerk at a local chain. And the coveted honor of the short story award was given to Colum Donnelly, a master at the Christian Brothers' Secondary School in Limerick. The checks, in the amount of two hundred pounds each, crossed hands in the ballroom of the Gresham Hotel, O'Connell Street, Dublin.

The Donnelly household was the scene of great celebration on the evening of the ceremony. Neighbors who had never read a word of Colum's work came by to congratulate "The Bard of Park," as they now referred to him, and to drink the black porter that Brendan distributed in foaming mugs. It was by great ado that Colum forced the money for the drink on his brother, but in the end he was successful. Brendan was short of cash lately, a point which he rarely discussed but which was evident in his nights spent by the hearth and not out and about the town.

When the crowds showed interest in leaving, Colum said that he would not hear of it. He insisted that they stay and sing and drink until "the dawn came up the Shannon." There was more porter on the way. (He had passed a fiver to Brendan, who left by the back door and was on his way to Gus Driscoll's for another barrel.) Some protested that they had work the next day, but others, caught up in the mood of frivolity, said, fuck work, that they'd be long enough dead. As a result, Colum was able to prolong the tenuous ecstasy of the moment.

When the crowds finally left a little after daybreak, he gave a twenty-pound note to his mother, and ten pounds each to Josie and Brendan. The women cried and his brother squeezed his neck so tightly that the blood seemed to burst to his head.

In the following weeks, the matter of the car was mentioned again and again. If he were going to buy one, Brendan told him, now was the time. All sorts of trades were being made in the heat of summer, and a person might be lucky. The private seller was the key, and Brendan had several in mind. The point was discussed each morning over the breakfast table and oftentimes as the two sat by the hearth in the late night. But little was done. It was as though a mother entertained her daughter with descriptions of some far-off wedding gown and described in rare detail its frills and ribbons and embroidery, sure that the reality would one day come, but content for the moment to allow it the status of a dream. As part of the stayed adventure, Brendan took his brother on a few jaunts out by Dooneas and Castleconnell, where he explained the function of each of the car's mechanical devices, and allowed the neophyte to test his agility on the winding and deserted country roads.

However, the game was short-lived. Near the end of the month, a young priest stopped by the Donnelly house. He had heard through a friend, a teacher at St. Michael's, that Colum might be in need of a car. He was on his way to the foreign missions and would have little use for the practically new Volkswagen left to him by his recently departed mother. In the matter of an hour, the transaction was closed, Colum half-reluctantly parting with the greater amount of his prize money, the parish credit union covering the balance, and the priest going happily on his way. Mrs. Donnelly had only one word to say. "The yard will be more cluttered with two jalopies," she said. "But this way, there'll be no fear that we'll be without a lift to Mass on a Sunday."

If the summer months were a backwater of study and self-contemplation for Colum, they were a time of frustration for Brendan. After Liam Daly's funeral, his role within the movement seemed to fall into a lull. He tried to convince himself that the entire summer period had been one of quiet in his sector. With the exception of a few minor skirmishes, of which he had not been part, the reported activity could only be considered humdrum.

Liam Daly's death still hung about his shoulders like a coat of mail. He inquired constantly as to the particulars of the boy's last hours. Yes, the women at Conway's on the Sandmall said, Liam had become very upset that Friday, irritated that the men would assume that the ambush had been pulled off by a foreigner. Yes, the RTE reporter, Michael Keough, attested, the young man was killed by his own hand, the shot having gone right up through the roof of his mouth and blown the top of his head to smithereens. His prints had been found on the Luger. And not the slightest suspicion of foul play. Brendan had remembered the correspondent's name from the broadcast on the night of Daly's death and, correctly assuming that the man would be staying at the costliest hotel in town, had sought out his room. Brendan would give no name, a fact that aroused the curiosity of the reporter. Was he a Provo? Of the terrorist faction? Would he be willing to tell his story? A large sum of money was proffered. This angered Brendan, and he pushed the man onto the sofa before hurriedly leaving the room and climbing down the back stairs of Cruise's Royal Hotel.

Chapter 23

The Volkswagen was in one way a curse. Whereas Brendan, because of his unpredictability, was never to be counted on for special trips and errands, except the sometimes lift to Mass on a Sunday, Colum was entirely a different matter. He was assailed with requests for lifts to the shops for ice cream, to the Baths for fresh air, and other pleas which tended to come at the height of his afternoon or evening writing sessions. He felt displeased, in a way, but knew that he would never intentionally hurt Josie's or his mother's feelings by refusing. Instead, he found himself leaving the house after lunch with his notebooks and spending the time down by the river. But he accomplished little there. The hot sun, too many young girls, and the fecund nature of the summer fields gave him little rest. There was no escape from the turgid life of the city. Like the retreatant who has scourged himself of his past sins, Colum felt restless, eager again for excitement. He had to admit that it was not totally due to his imposed expulsion from the house. It had been coming on for some time. It became more difficult each day to concentrate on his own work and easier to take pleasure in that of others. He read again Joyce's *Ulysses*, especially Molly's soliloquy, Gide's *The Counterfeiters*, and Melville's *Typee*. After a time, even the books were not enough, their pages fluttering in the breeze as he stared far off towards the hazy summit of Mount Keeper.

On the first Friday night in July, he drove to a dance in Pallas Green. He had gone there earlier in the year and it was on that occasion that he had met Ellen Sullivan. The night out would do him good, he felt, and the car with its assurance of mobility and independence gave him a special confidence. No more would it be necessary to cut short the fun of the dance to wait sometimes for hours in the draughty station for the train back to the city.

He danced most of the waltzes, sitting out only those songs of the come-all-ye class. He had no mind for mediocrity, now. In the second to last dance he was paired with a girl from Kilkenny who also happened to be a secondary school teacher. She had spent the earlier part of the summer at home and was visiting "down country" for a few days before returning to the "insane asylum" where she taught Elocution and English. When he mentioned his name, she paused and then almost shouted, "You're the story writer from *The Press* and *Times*. I've read you! A little dirty now and again. Right?"

"Well . . ."

"More power to you, Colum."

Sheila was nothing less than a mad hatter. She had opinions on almost every subject. Birth control. The use of chrism in Church services during an oil embargo. The North. The poor quality of wadding in cigarette filters. The plight of the National University. And it all tumbled out into the dank air of the dance hall. Colum was fascinated by her. He enjoyed especially the attention she gave his hobby, writing. In the middle of the floor, she bombarded him with questions on plot, on the writer's knack for making a place seem real with only a few words, on the closeness of fiction to reality, on the possibility of putting her in a story. He laughed. He was into his barrow with her.

After the dance, they drove to a small pub in Caherconlish. It was near closing time so he ordered three short whiskies and a pint. Sheila requested a Pim Number One, but the countryman behind the bar had never heard of such a concoction. She had a Carlsberg ale, instead.

When they were seated, he said, "I'm sorry that they didn't have your drink."

"Oh, that's all right. I just asked for the fancy drink so that I'd get that old fellow's goat."

"What?"

"You have to now and again, or they'll sink into the Middle Ages. So far as some of these thicks are concerned, Brian Boru was a grand Catholic family man who died yesterday. They need awakening, and it's up to us to give them the pin in the arse."

He smiled and gulped one of his whiskies.

"Seriously," she said. "I don't believe in bombings and slaughter, but the Prods up North aren't all wrong. We down here in the Republic have been lulled to sleep for too long, the priests and nuns having a grand time making up the tunes. We're free of them now, at least in some quarters. Our first emancipation was from John Bull. Our second must be from all the Holy Marys of this forsaken bit of North Atlantic rock. Do you know that we had a nun where I went to school whose greatest worry was that she'd be compelled to fart during the Consecration! One of the girls on my floor overheard her in Confession . . ."

He spilled his Guinness all over his shirt. Finally, when he gained his composure, he said, "I know what you mean. Hands out of the pocket for fear that fornication may result!"

"Oh, Christ."

"So the motto is 'Antagonize'?"

"It has been for some time. Where have you been, Colum?"

"Away."

"You see, it's a game. Nobody gets seriously hurt, but ideas, at least, are tossed about, and new things happen. It beats the boredom."

"Change for change's sake?"

"Right."

"Seems like a good diversion."

When the pub closed, he drove her to her lodgings in Bruff. She invited him in. He surprised himself when he said, "No. I'd better not. It's a long drive back."

"You could stay for the night," she said.

"But, alas, our reputations!"

"Nobody knows us here."

"Really, I should get back. I have an appointment in the morning," he lied.

"Well, will I see you again?"

"Yes. Let's make a date for the Friday after this one."

"I won't be here. I'll be back preparing for school."

"I'd forgotten."

"Don't we all!"

"Why don't I come to Kilkenny? We could make a weekend of it."

"Terrific!"

He put his arm about her shoulder and kissed her. Almost casually, she reached behind and undid the snap of her brassiere. He fondled her breasts. But after a few moments he leaned back. It was not that Sheila Collins was unattractive—far from it. But some quality in the drift of things cried out to him to halt. He had been too eager before. He remembered with bitterness Rayana's smug smile as she had reached between his thighs and mechanically relieved him of his seed. And now with this strong drink on him . . . No. He would wait. He would not risk looking like a fool again. Ever.

He kissed her. "Friday after next," he said.

Sheila did not reply but put her arms about his waist and squeezed him tightly.

By the time he reached the village of Ballyneety, he had swerved off the macadam several times. The drink and its companion, sleep, played strange tricks on him. He told himself, at times, that he could close his eyes and catnap while still keeping the car on the road. On other occasions, the reality of driving extended itself into a dream of driving the same road in broad sunlight. He played both games on and off until he reached the outskirts of the city. He was almost home. Just a few more miles by way of back roads.

Suddenly, he realized that the blue flashing light in his rearview mirror was no mirage. When he finally stopped (he had dallied with the notion of escape, at first), the navy-uniformed Gardai were far from polite.

"Out!" the taller of the two shouted. "Hand over the keys."

Colum looked into the gawkish face of the Guard. The scenario was right from the telly. Two loutish policemen . . .

"The keys!" the shorter man shouted.

Colum imagined that the pavement rose up and crashed into his face. His stomach twirled inside of him. He closed his eyes to gain his equilibrium. He said, "What is this? Who gives you thicks the authority . . ."

Later, he remembered only the sudden pain as the truncheon struck his skull. Then there was a blackness, an uneasy void in which he sensed that he was being thrown backwards and forwards with the motion of the police van. However, he did not see light again until he was pitched headlong into a gas-lit jail cell at William Street Barracks, where he remained until Brendan came for him in the late morning.

Out in the bustle of William Street, Colum said, "How did you get me out?"

"Ah, I told them that you'd just gotten out of the Brothers.
I said that if they charged you, you'd lose your job and
everything."

"Then what?"

"One of the Guards wanted to go on with the charges. But
the other talked him out of it. They agreed that the experience most certainly taught you a lesson."

"A lesson? What am I, some bloody child?"

Colum was sullen on the way through the old parish. At
Dwyer Bridge, Brendan turned to him and said, "How was it
in there? What do they do to people?"

"What you'd expect. They shove them in with tinkers,
whoremasters, thieves, and God knows who else. They let
them share a cell that is fit for four but houses sixteen, while
at the same time, the rest of the row is empty. They give
them a hole in the ground to shit and piss in. And they feed
them slop for food."

Brendan's foot eased off the accelerator. "Did they give
anyone a beating?" he said.

"Yes, one of your lads, I think. Someone said that he'd
been part of a raid on a Guard station in Croom."

"A raid? I never heard anything about that."

"They took him out. You could hear his screams."

"Rubber hose."

"I guess."

"And I suppose that he came back without a mark on
him?"

"He did. But the poor devil couldn't move. He was all
hunched up."

"There'll be murder over this, you'll see."

"The rotten fuckers. And they call this a Christian country."

The railway gates were open for a change, and the Morris
Minor sped on through and up the hill towards the Bonard
Corner.

Chapter 24

The long sultry days of summer were coming to an end. Brendan could feel it in the night breezes and in the hint of morning frost on the fields. He dreaded winter, especially the one that was coming on. He had lately begun to see himself as ordinary, as the young aimless character who had gone from job to job, a year before, having been dishonorably discharged from the L.D.F. (He had beaten a bullying sergeant with his fists.) It was at that time that the Provos had accepted him with open arms. He remembered the blood oaths, the training, the indoctrination, the ambushes—and the great bashes that followed, and the admiration of the men about him. He had been more than one of the boyos. He had been a man apart, looked up to for his skill and fervor. Or had that really been the case? he asked himself in these droll days. Was he being jeered at instead of being praised? Was he regarded by those in command as part of the mob of which Riordan had spoken, to be used and manipulated like a puppet? The thoughts seared him when he recalled how little attention had been paid to him in recent weeks, especially after the last meeting he had attended. At that time, he had openly condemned the killing of the British ambassador, Mr. Ewart-Biggs. Standing on his chair, he said, "Jesus Christ! We know he looked like Lord Snoot, with his monocle and Oxford accent. But was that any reason to slaughter the poor old fool in broad daylight? Don't we have any feelings at all, are we a bunch of mad . . ."

The vehemence of the shouted response startled him. "Terrorists!" one screamed. "We're fucking terrorists and not kiddies playing cowboy."

"If it's too hot for your soft feelings, Donnelly, why don't you get your arse out? Become a social worker. Be another pal of a guy like Kojak."

He lunged at the last tormentor and the man fled the hall while a few bystanders held Brendan back. The word "terrorists" flogged at his mind. Certainly he believed in violence but not in useless murder. That was not the role of the movement. Its mission was to rid the country of scoundrels. But talk was cheap. He was sure that it would never come to outright killing in Munster. It could only be expected from the Dublin guttersnipes. They'd slit their mothers' throats for a ha'penny. It had always been that way, even in the Troubles.

That had been the last meeting he attended. Two following sessions had been called without his knowledge. When he complained to Buckley, the response was casual. "Ah, they forgot you, Brendie," he said. "You live so far out, the young lads passing the word must have put you on the cuff. Probably hoped that you'd hear, anyway." He could not put his finger on it, but he felt as plainly as the nose on his face that behind all the neglect was the image of Riordan himself. He cursed his dead-man's face. Hadn't the old man given out to him that day about bringing novices into the organization? Wasn't that enough? Forgive and forget? Why did it have to drag on like this? And even if Buckley had passed on his curse to Riordan—and he knew Raef better than to betray him like that—well, wasn't the old man human? Didn't he understand feeling and anger?

The long uneventful days unsettled him, too, in other ways. The face of Liam was before his eyes morning and night. This was mainly due to his avoidance of "The Field" and the Daly household. What would he tell Liam's mother? Invent an intrigue that had no basis in fact? And what then? The case was closed, but he didn't have the heart to tell her.

In the beginning, he often thought that he saw Liam on the street or passing in a car. Surely these were illusions. But what if it were all a plot, a ruse by the Guards to . . . What was he talking about? Hadn't he seen the lad's corpse there on the bed, bandaged in death? The boy had been declared officially dead. He was in his grave. It was a fact.

Later, his preoccupation changed its focus. His thoughts

drifted back again to the insanity of the death, its defiance of all that he had accepted as normal and possible. It was then that he took to following people who wore jackets the color of Liam's or hats that were pressed out in the same cocked mold as that of his friend.

On one occasion, he ran after a man on Perry Street, followed him all the way to the docks, and finally pinned him against the Tedcastle wall. "Where did you get that topcoat?" he shouted. "Where did you get it?"

The man looked about in terror. "Nowhere," he said. "Nowhere."

"Tell me or I'll take your life!"

"Nowhere. I bought it at Pashie Brown's over a year ago. For fifteen bob. I didn't steal it. I didn't. Are you a detective sergeant?"

Brendan released the man. He would have to take hold of himself. He looked closely at the coat. It was nowhere near the color of Liam's gabardine.

"I'm sorry," he said. I'm really sorry."

The man sighed deeply with relief. He put out his hand and touched Brendan. "Tell me, son," he said, "did the coat you're looking for belong to someone that's dead?"

Brendan was incredulous. "It did," he admitted.

"I knew it. It's part of the trick that death plays on our old minds. It happened the same with myself when my oldest boy, Seamus, was drownded . . ."

Brendan leaned against the wall and allowed the man to explain the phenomenon. The words had a way of soothing his nightmarish fears.

Chapter 25

Colum could not remember a storm such as this. It had given no warning at all, but had edged its way inconspicuously up the Shannon, hiding behind the shelter of ships on the horizon and the great chimney stacks and flour mills far down in the mouth of the river. But now it was upon the city, its rain pouring from the vast darkness above the streets and shops and scurrying crowds.

He tried to cross to the Augustinian Church, but feeling the heavy drops on his face, he decided instead to take shelter in the familiar shop behind him. He needed typing paper, anyway. He might as well pick it up right now. There was no use making another trip back in.

Mahony's Book Store was crowded with grumbling shoppers. A terrible storm altogether, they said. None like it since 1954 when children were lifted bodily out of the river and thrown against the strand, when one of the bolts struck a misfortunate horse on the pier and drove him stark mad. . . . Colum had heard the details many times over. He pushed his way to the rear of the shop.

Before reaching the stationery counter, he noticed that the "Literary Rack," in the alcove to the right, contained many new titles. He forgot momentarily about his errand and quickly walked to the wooden frame. Ah, yes. Old books to the great outside world, but new to this forgotten place. *The Hamlet. A Separate Peace. The Man Who Died. At-Swim, Two Birds. Humboldt's Gift.*

He lifted the Faulkner book from its place and turned to the Flem section. He began to read aloud:

> All they saw now was that they had a new
> blacksmith—a man who was not lazy, whose intentions
> were good and who was accommodating and
> unfailingly pleasant and even generous, yet in
> whom there was a definite limitation of physical
> co-ordination beyond which design and plan and pattern
> all vanished, distintegrated into dead
> components of pieces of wood and iron straps and vain
> tools.

He felt a hand on his left arm. He turned suddenly to see a gaunt gray man stand beside him, too close for mere accident. But before he could shift his position, the man spoke. "A strange lad, that Faulkner," he said. "Almost Irish in his layerings of language. They say that he often saw Joyce in Paris but was too awed to approach him."

Colum was stunned. Someone discussing Faulkner *in Limerick!* "Have you read *The Sound and the Fury?*" he asked sheepishly.

"Oh, yes. Quentin and his watch. Caddy and her soiled knickers."

The man extended his hand. "I'm certain you're Colum Donnelly," he said. "Unless my eyes failed me the other day up at Mount St. Lawrence, you were with Brendan, your brother."

Colum was dumbfounded. He stared into the sallow face, noticing immediately the unnatural set of the eyes. A menacing aura seemed to emanate from the man, but one that was not unattractive in its own seductive way. He knew now why his brother and the others were drawn to this ogre, this tall branch of flesh and bone. He knew, too, that he should excuse himself, say that his name was not Donnelly at all, not anybody that this man had a knowledge of, that this lone man was alien to all he had known to this point and all that perhaps he hoped to know in the gamut of his life. And yet, another side of him dictated his actions. It said that this was no ghost, that here stood only a man with dead eyes, in a dead face, garbed in the black of priests. Hadn't he conquered such nonsense before, hadn't he rallied against it? Certainly he had. It was a ruse, a mirage fashioned to keep all those of weak heart at bay or under its spell. "Mr. Riordan," he said, "I had no idea that when Brendan told me he could arrange a meeting . . ."

"Neither did Brendan, I'm afraid. I've looked forward to this pleasure."

"So have I. So have I."

Riordan stood back from the light and seemed to lean against an imaginary post. He looked at Colum, taking in every aspect of him. Then he said, "It's awfully crowded here. Could we go somewhere to have a little chat?"

"Anywhere."

"Laffey's pub."

"Grand."

The rain and darkness were increasing. The city was swollen with muddy pools and assorted debris.

Farrell delivered the drinks and left without a word. Colum and Riordan regarded each other in the half-light. The older man was the first to speak. "Well, Colum," he said, "as I was saying to your hotheaded brother, Brendan, I've read and admired your work. Some very fine stories indeed. A marvelous toying with what is real and what isn't. And recently the vast change in tone. And, of course, the resulting award. Congratulations!"

"Thank you."

"It's as if your perspective has changed immensely."

"Well . . ."

"You've come out of yourself. Things have happened to you, haven't they?"

"I suppose."

"I guessed as much. Your stories have more objectivity now. More of a sense of fine distance. Your characters are your puppets. You have removed your feeling from their nature. They are no longer hindered by being masks for yourself."

Colum was amazed by the man's insight. Was he a writer himself? He certainly knew the bones beneath the flesh.

Riordan seemed to have read his thoughts when he said, "How do I know so much? I'll tell you. I, too, am an inventor of characters, particularly one."

Colum was puzzled. "Who would that be?" he said.

Riordan smiled. "Oh, a powerful one indeed. A true romantic."

"Who?"

" 'The Renegade.' "

"Yourself!"

"Ah, yes." Riordan reached and touched Colum on the knee.

A violent repulsion for the man ran through him. He felt the drink sour in his throat. He knew that he should slap the hand from his leg, but his arms remained limp at his sides. Was he the pawn of all the Christian Brothers' admonitions against immorality? Or was he the man of the world who tolerated all forms of aberration, and was above them, safe because of his sober reason and intellect? He found himself rooted to the chair, his curiosity blotting out all argument for leaving. "I don't quite see," he said.

Riordan took his hand away. "Tell me," he said, "who do they say that I am?"

Colum breathed heavily. Riordan's manner confused him. "I'm not familiar . . ."

"What have you heard about me other than my imprisonment at Long Kesh? Where did I come from? Who were my parents?"

Colum looked at the bartender. His back was to them. "Okay," he said. "Let's see. First of all, it's said that your mother was German. Right?"

"Correct. And the Irish have always had a great love for things Prussian. They are the only ones left who still believe in Hitler's Master Race. Organization. Technology. Cruel discipline. Not having any of these things themselves, they adore it in others. Go on."

Colum began to see the drift and became eager to explore further. "You were born in the States. But educated at Oxford."

"A curious combination, really. The inhabitants of this island have a grand yen for Americans, their money, their clothes, their outspokenness, their freedom. But they by no chance respect their intelligence."

"What about the scientists? Von Braun? Einstein?"

"So far as the Irish are concerned, they're transplanted Germans."

"Right. Right."

"Having a German mother wasn't quite enough. The second part of the antidote was Oxford. To the peasant it stands for aristocracy. A superior university system. An education painfully in advance of anything on this bit of rock. Just produce the parchment that says you attended, say, Exeter College, and where does that put you?"

"On top."

"Of course. The very top."

"I see."

"And say that your stay at Oxford was nothing more than a brief two months one summer, and that your mother was a German peasant without an ounce of education, and that you lived in the States for only one month before crossing over into Canada, would it matter one iota?"

"No."

"Ah, there you have it!"

Colum leaned on the table in front of them. "Your life story was invented to suit the mob," he said.

"No. But the essential highlights were emphasized."

"Packaged."

"To use an American term."

Colum sipped his small brandy. "Why are you telling me this?" he said. "I could expose you."

"You wouldn't."

"Why?"

"Because we're in the same trade, essentially. And our reward is the same."

"What is that?"

"Control. The ability to move pawns in a private game of life. To call one hero and the other villain, at will."

Farrell had arrived with two more brandies and a jug of fresh water. He suddenly pulled a lighter from his apron and lit Riordan's cigarette. "Thank you, Farrell," the old man said.

When the bartender had left, Colum asked, "Are you telling me that you are indifferent to the speeches, the slogans, the songs . . ."

"They leave me cold."

"I'm still a bit puzzled. This is a religious war, they tell us. A war between Catholic and Protestant. Religion is at the heart of it, medieval primitive religion. You're at the heart of it. Musn't you be one and the same, or at least one tainted by the other?"

Riordan laughed, and Colum saw for the first time the stained teeth behind the lips. "Tell me," the older man said, "do you come away from your puppet show feeling the same emotions that you have assigned to your toys? Are you the heart or head of your performance?"

"The head."

"As those of us in command are. Doesn't it seem strange to you that when you look closely you notice that this is a religious war with no religious leaders at its head—a religious war, too important to be left to churchmen?"

"The leaders do not share the ideals of the led."

"Precisely. Did you ever notice as a lad that when your brave parish priest spoke of the dignity of poverty and the honor of deprivation that he himself slept in a shack or ate the scraps off someone's table?"

"I didn't."

"Patriotism is for the simpleminded. All leaders give it lip service. Arafat. Idi Amin. Carter."

"A myth."

"A facade for the general public that is superstitious, sentimental, and insecure. And one also for a greater part of the old guard within the movement."

Colum knew that Riordan was including Brendan in the latter category. He should have felt anger at this, but he didn't. He saw Riordan scrutinize him. He said, "Your whole organization would fall apart on the truth?"

"Yes. If we once admitted that we were anarchists only, we would no longer wield power. And if we took the battle into the economic sphere alone, then the fight wouldn't be worth the cost, and there'd be a compromise in the morning. But when the cause is religious and patriotic, compromise and conciliation are out of the question."

Colum could feel his heart beat against his ribs. He looked furtively about the pub. A man sitting with a young child in the corner. Farrell lazily drying glasses. The rain beating down outside. Nothing out of the ordinary. No harm at all.

It seemed that a long time passed before Colum broke the silence and said, "Why do you think that I would be interested in joining you?"

"I just have a feeling. It would be the supreme freedom for you—arranging facts in their appropriate colors, using your gift of rhetoric to show another angle to all that exists . . ."

"Propaganda?"

"I know of little else that is so akin to fiction."

Colum saw the implications. "What exactly would I do?" he said.

Riordan was smiling again. "Oh, it'd be simple," he said. "You'd work right under me, be my right-hand man, as it were. You would be fed all the same information that comes to me, now, reports of raids, Government searches, police traps—the lot. You, then, would give our version to the people."

"Through your newspaper?"

"Cumas."

"I've read it once or twice. Brendan used to bring it . . ."

"Then you see why we need real talent so desperately. It's a gathering of hacks—not that some functionaries aren't needed."

Colum remembered the badly printed circular that he had often found by the hearth. The wild accusations. The out-and-out fantasy. The dredging up of old glories and past accomplishments. The poor grammar.

Riordan saw that Colum's eagerness was fading. "Poor Cumas," he said. "But poor no longer."

"Why is that?"

"We have received over half a million dollars from our various clubs and organizations in the States. A newspaper is what we need, they tell us. A polished articulate outlet of news. Those Yanks know the value of print, I needn't tell you."

"My name would be given?"

"Oh, no. This way you could say anything you wanted to. Attack any thing or any one. Never the slightest fear of libel or arrest. Nothing but complete control."

"Where would I work?"

"Kilkenny. We have a press near that town. It is a district of little activity."

Colum paused. "And the pay?" he said.

"Pay? We'd double what you're making now."

"I see." His face flushed.

It was overwhelming. What more could a writer ask for but that he be allowed to write and be well paid into the bargain? No more chalky classrooms. Sweaty bodies. Arrogance. The absolute terror of facing the sea of ignorance each morning. Then, again, there was the matter of leaving home, taking up in a new town where he knew nobody—except Sheila! He had forgotten that she lived in Kilkenny. But still, she was a relative stranger. What about Mama? Josie? Even Brendan? And what about Brother Roland? He owed *him* a great deal. "I don't know," he said. "It's an enticing proposition. But I'd really have to . . ."

"By all means, think about it. We want you to be perfectly sure. You'll do a better job as editor if you're happy and contented."

"Editor?"

"Yes. Take a week. A month, if you want. Let me know whenever you're ready."

"Through Brendan?"

"No!" Riordan's voice was harsh. "I'm afraid that we must exclude him from all this. Absolute secrecy. You see what I mean?"

"Yes."

"It's for your protection as well as our own."

"To be sure."

Why was it that this last detail excited him more than all the rest? The emotion was almost identical to that which he had felt as a child when he had continuously outsmarted Brendan in the silly game of hide-and-seek.

"Well, anyway," Riordan said, "you can let me know at this address." He handed Colum a slip of yellow paper.

He did not open it, but slipped the note into his vest pocket. "I will," he said.

Riordan looked towards the light of the doorway. "It hasn't cleared," he said. "We'd better have one more for the road, a *deoc an dorais*, as they say."

He made no protest though he knew that he was feeling the influence of the strong drink. He'd have to be careful. He couldn't be having a repeat of his recent bad fortune. He tightened as he remembered the scowling faces of the police.

"This country and its cursed rain," Riordan said absently.

"What?"

"The rain outside."

"Oh."

"I remember once another storm such as this. I was no more than First Communion age. My mother and I had stood for hours in a Salvation Army soup line in Montreal. Oh, how it rained all that morning! And when we reached the end of the queue, they said that the soup was gone and to come back tomorrow. Bastards!"

Colum was embarrassed by the sudden strange emotion in the man. He silently lifted his glass to his mouth.

Riordan seemed to catch himself. His voice suddenly changed. "But we have to be content with it," he said. "Rain. Rain. It wouldn't be Ireland without it."

"That's a fact."

Chapter 26

On the Friday night before the opening of school, Colum drove to Kilkenny. He made it plain, on leaving the house, that he was taking a few days rest. It would do him good, he said, to make the long drive, give him time for his own thoughts before starting school. Though all agreed, his mother and Josie had reservations. He had better watch the strong drink, the old woman said, and Josie, beside her, almost ruined it all by asking if he had a new girlfriend tucked away in Kilkenny. His face reddened. But Brendan stood between him and the women. "Come on," he said. "I'll help you to the car with your suitcase."

In the yard, Brendan said, "Colum, take the Annacotty road. You'll be safer. Not so many Guards on that one."

"Okay."

"When will you be back?"

"Sunday, maybe."

"*Is* there a bird?—I shouldn't ask."

Colum smiled. "There is," he said.

"Not the Yank?"

"Oh, no." He lowered his voice to a whisper. "She went back to her old man."

"Father?"

"Husband."

"Husband!"

Colum watched the concern and awe in Brendan's eyes. And suddenly he wanted to tell him here and now of Riordan's offer. He imagined the pride that would fill the face opposite him, the shouts, the arms about the neck. But he stopped. He only knew that the thought came as he looked across the yard at Brendan's Morris Minor, unused of late, covered with dust, marooned in the corner with the rusted bicycle of their father.

Sheila's flat was situated in the north of the city of

Kilkenny where the river Nore drifts lazily through the green fields then suddenly angles south through houses that have long lost their immaculate whitewash veneer and given way to a tawdry grayness matching that of the rest of the city. But once inside her door, Colum found her two rooms and kitchen to be not dismal at all but comfortable in their niceties—a color telly, a record player, a fridge, and a tiny rack of French wines.

It was not until Sheila left the parlor with his suitcase that the reality of his position dawned on him. Here he was, a man who only five months before spent his evenings in prayer before a curtained tabernacle. Even then his mind had often drifted off into sexual fantasies, though he had told himself at the time that they were wrong. But perhaps that was due to the fact that he felt they would never be realized, not in a lifetime. How easily it all had come about. All a man had to do was reach out and say, "Come to me," and even in stodgy old Ireland, it was there, there at his fingertips. He wondered if it were part of the times, or if it had always existed. For his father? For the men before *him?*

When Sheila returned he said, "Where will we go tonight? A dance? A picture?—after which I buy you dinner, of course."

"Nonsense. I wouldn't hear of it. I have everything prepared. Chops. Browned potatoes. Trifle. Wine. Everything."

"Well," he said, "what can I say in the face of such persuasion? But you're sure?"

"Certain. I should have been as persuasive the last time. You wouldn't have had the trouble you did."

"Isn't that the truth!" How many times he had regretted turning down her offer. The thought worked now as an antidote to the slight apprehension that had been gradually building inside him. It quieted his fears. Though he did not believe in superstition, he allowed that a quirk of fate was involved here, that it would be unnatural to oppose it. It reminded him of the games he'd played as a child. How often he had raced a car or a dog and, having won, negotiated his fate with whoever it was that controlled those things. He would live long. He would marry the prettiest girl in Limerick. He would never suffer pain . . . He settled deeper into the sofa.

Towards the middle of the extravagant meal, Sheila's voice lost some of its good spirits. "This is my Last Supper, in a way," she said. "School starting next week, a lot of preparation to be done this one. Oh, how I hate it."

"So do I. I dread it." He did not feel it necessary to even hint at Riordan's offer. It was for himself, nobody else. The secrecy of it had grown in him, though he had made no decision as yet. "Perhaps," he added, "I should say the words of Consecration over this 'fruit of the vine.' "

"Don't. You've gone from the old beliefs?"

"Yes. I have sentimental feelings towards them, at times. They remind me of my childhood. The early winter mornings serving Mass. The ritual that drowned out the pain of rational thought. The wonder of the Christmas crib . . ." The wine was making him maudlin. He was sure that he felt tears welling up inside. He stopped.

"I've given the religion up, too," she said. "But like yourself, I have a certain nostalgia. It's not always easy to be free from the rigmarole. Sometimes the world of objects is as frustrating as the one of images. I am not strong enough to accept the inevitable worm . . ."

He caught the hysterical note and quickly changed the subject. "A delicious feast," he said. "I don't think that I've ever had a better one."

"Oh, go on with you!"

"No. Really."

Sheila lit a fire in the grate, but also turned up the gas heat. She said that one was not enough by itself. It needed the other. And late in the night it was as cold as winter in the flat.

Colum looked at his watch. Midnight. He swallowed the dregs of his wine. "Can I help you with the crockery?" he said.

"No. I'll leave it. I'll be up early to cook you a big

breakfast. Do you like black pudding?"

"Devour it."

"Grand."

After she had come around the table and kissed him, it was easy to run his hands under her jumper and below the rim of her skirt, simple to lead her in the direction of the bedroom, no bother to flop her down on the patched quilt. No more deprivation. No more holding back. No more games. There was a power in this, a semblance that one was outside the natural element, drifting in some rosy expanse of space. With each movement of his limbs, the sensuous aura spread until he was almost not able to control it.

Sheila pulled back. "Colum," she said, "I have to tell you. I'm no prize. I'm not an old hat at this, as I pretended. Two awkward times. Once with a boy when I was in secondary school. Another with an Indian student from Trinity."

"Don't. There's no need to. I'm not . . ."

"But I don't want to spoil everything."

"You won't."

Her voice broke, and he saw tears on her face. He kissed her mouth. He felt no urgency, no great demand to perform. Her terror had disarmed his own fears.

Carefully he removed his clothing. He then gently undid the clasp of her skirt. He felt calm, as though he had followed a long circuitous path and found at its end a place of no great splendor, but, nonetheless, of satisfying and sufficient dimension.

An hour later he lay awake. Sheila slept beside him. He looked down at her schoolgirl's face. He experienced no desire now. But he could see the sense which it would make again after the night was gone and his body and emotions had replenished themselves with food and images. The old lie (or was it truth?) perpetrated by one cell upon the other. God! The magnitude of the procreative plot chilled him. It was here that man must surely catch a glimpse of the universe's indifference. Here at this center, where the body was as body, as breasts, as limbs, as hair, as flesh. And he thought of all the sermons and condemnations and chants thrust out against this thing that lay harmless beneath his touch. Man's fear of his own erotic nature. But he put the serious thoughts from his mind. This was not the time!

He snuggled closer to Sheila. She uttered a small cry in her sleep and turned her face from him.

Chapter 27

Had Sheila her way, Colum would never have left her flat. They had spent most of the short weekend inside—he found that she was as conscious of public opinion as himself. But she had a secondary motive, too. Despite her earlier fears, she now displayed an insatiable sexual curiosity and cajoled him into experimenting with every twist and turn she had heard about or read of or seen practiced on the screen. He was not a reluctant companion in this, but when Sunday came, he felt tired, enough being enough of a good thing. Of course, he promised to return after the beginning of school. They'd see the city the next time, picnic down by the Nore, visit the old cathedral . . .

He was relaxed as he turned the Volkswagen west in the direction of home. It was good to be neither here nor there, to be suspended. He laughed as he thought of Sheila's curiosity and felt the bump on the back of his head—he had fallen out of bed as a result of one of her unusual games. She was a character, indeed.

It was late when he arrived home, and all were asleep. He parked the car on the road, and once inside the house, doused the lights, undressing himself in the darkness. There was no need to have them wait on him with tea and food; he'd last the night without that. And, anyway, he was in no mood for giving any exploits. He'd have to do a little thinking beforehand.

The following morning, when he had related as much as possible of his weekend holiday—he told them that he had stayed with another teacher—he sat sipping his tea at the table. Brendan was seated opposite him. Their mother was out of earshot.

"How was it?" Brendan said.

"Oh, Jesus!"

"A wild caper?"

"You've never seen the likes of it in all your born days."

"You look a little pale."

"Lack of sunshine."

"You fucker. You crazy mad fucker."

Just then their mother interrupted. "Colum," she said, "I almost forgot. You had a letter from the Brothers, Saturday, when you were gone. Here. I put it up on the mantel behind the china dogs."

"Your full appointment," Brendan said.

"Oh, God, you're right. That's what it is, I'll bet."

Colum reached behind the ornaments and found the letter. It was from Sexton Street, all right. From Brother Roland.

He opened it with his thumbnail. But as he did so, he felt his stomach turn at the thought of school.

He began to read aloud, the words not having their full effect until he reached the middle of the page. Suddenly he dropped the letter to the ground and walked out the back door.

"Jesus, Mary, and Joseph!" his mother cried. "What's happened? What's the matter?"

Brendan picked up the crumpled note. He read aloud:

DEAR COLUM:

It is with great regret that I must write to you concerning this matter. As you are aware, you were hired on a temporary basis in the spring,

preliminary to a full appointment this fall. However, an
event has occurred which drastically affects our
plans. As you know, Thursday was our last day for
enrollments. Well, we received the shock of our
lives—the number of boys was down by almost a
hundred. I can only speculate that this tragedy
was caused by the growing popularity of the Technical
Institute and its programmes. Alas, a classical
education seems to be a thing of the past. Of course,
you can see where all of this puts us in regards
to your position with the school. As it stands, Mr.
Delahunty, our senior master, will take over
your classes until he retires next summer. God granting
some stability, you will be the first called to fill
his vacancy.

Again, my sincere regrets. You will, to be sure, receive
only the highest commendations from this
quarter. I wish you every success.

> I remain,
> sincerely yours,
> REV. BROTHER ROLAND O'BRIEN, C.B.S.

"What does it all mean?" the mother asked.
"That he's out," Brendan answered.
"Out of the Brothers?"
"Out of a job."
He reached for his hat. "I'm going after him," he said.

Chapter 28

When Brendan finally caught up with his brother,
Colum had already crossed by Poll Lucais and was
headed towards the Shannon Fields. "Wait,
Colum!" he shouted, but the other kept on walking at a brisk
pace as though he had not heard a word.

At last he reached him and put his arm on his shoulder.

"Listen," he said. "Listen. Don't let the stupid thing worry you. There are plenty of jobs around for those with your education. It's oafs like me that have to be worried. All you have to do is look in the paper. As a matter of fact, I'll show you tonight when I get the *Leader*."

Colum slipped out from under the heavy arm. "No," he said, "that won't be necessary. I don't give a fuck about the job. I never did. It's their hypocrisy that eats on me."

Brendan paused. His eyes blinked against the sunlight. "Still," he said, "there's not much they could do, considering."

"Considering what? Considering that my training far surpasses that of Delahunty, the old codger. Or any of them, for that matter. But I've got to be the one that gets the door. You're fucking aye. Give the sack to the new and bright, and keep the dull and maimed on forever to perpetuate the already entrenched ignorance."

Brendan was puzzled. It had been years since he'd seen a tantrum like this from Colum. And he remembered well the last occasion. Their father had put his hand on the boy's throat and said, "So help me Jesus, I'll take your very life if I hear another word out of you." Of course, the mother had grasped the squirming child from the old man's clutch and coddled him. At this moment, Brendan understood his father's anger.

"I'm going to walk a bit," Colum said. "Tell Mama that I'll be back late. I'll get something to eat at one of the cafés in town."

"Tell her yourself."

"Fuck you then."

Brendan's hands shot forward and grasped his brother by the lapels. "Take care," he said, "that you don't ever use that tone of voice to another one of your own."

"Why? Are you my father?"

"You'll think father when I finish with you."

"Let go of me. I have business in town."

"What business?"

"I have to go to the post office."

Brendan relaxed his grip. "If you're going to draw out money from your post office book, there's no need . . ."

"I'm not short of money. I don't need anybody's money. I'm posting a letter to accept a job."

"What?"

"I have a new job already. Twice the pay, as a matter of fact. I'll set all those who crossed me on their heels."

Brendan could see the scowl on his brother's face. The narrowness of the eyes. The vindictive tone of the voice. He felt as though he were facing a stranger, a foreigner to this place of easy words and imperturbable peace. "Wait," he said, trying desperately to bring back the familiar image of Colum as gentle and at the most just sporadically peevish. But it was impossible. The other was acting like a cornered animal.

"Yes," Colum said, and laughed. "They'll see. My day is coming."

"See what? What are you talking about?"

"You'll see, by God. I'll show the lot."

Then he turned, and he seemed to dance rather than walk off towards the headlands of the Shannon Fields.

Chapter 29

In the first week of September, Brendan accepted a job. It was offered to him by a friend of Seoirse's, and though at first he was reluctant to take it, he nonetheless realized that new assignments from within the movement were not forthcoming. The job at the Guinness Barrel Yard was not to be laughed at. In the first place, he considered that he would be warm and dry all winter long, and in the second, he would always have enough free porter to wet his whistle and calm his nerves. What more could a man ask for?

The men at the Barrel Yard took instantly to Brendan. His good nature and his affinity to hard work made him a favorite within days. And his tenor voice, which brightened up their after-work stout sessions at Quilligan's pub, in no way hindered him.

The foreman, John Shanahan, admired his new laborer. He saw immediately that Brendan possessed great energy. He put that quality to use, never allowing it to weave itself into boredom or sullenness. He worked him on the jetty, in the storeroom, on the barges, and even, on occasion, though it was not permitted by union regulations, he allowed him to drive the lorries between the unloading dock and the locks section of the canal.

On one of his trips in the lorry, Brendan met Brian Jaggers, an ex-R.A.F. man, now living with his wife and six children in the Abbey, the central area of the parish. At first, Brendan avoided him because he was an Englishman, and because, by working at Guinness's, he surely deprived an Irishman of the job. Or so Brendan told himself as he stood by and watched the expert driver maneuver his lorry into the tightest spots or jump from his seat the moment someone needed a lift or a shove. But gradually, the respect of the other men for Jaggers eroded his initial dislike. Jaggers was a Protestant, to be sure, they said, but his children were at eight o'clock Mass every morning, their faces shined, their clothes spotless. Jaggers was a private man, but when it came down to a tight spot, he could be counted on for a ready hand or a few quid out of his pay envelope. A born gentleman, they said, which was more praise than could be given to a lot on this side of the Irish Sea.

Brendan, however, rarely worked side by side with the lorry driver. Other laborers were assigned to him and they protected this privilege by seldom missing a day for fear that someone else might grab for the job. But just such an opening did occur, a few weeks after Brendan was hired. Old Dinzie Shea, Jaggers's cabman, died of a heart attack. The vacancy commanded great speculation on the part of the men.

The morning after the funeral, Shanahan called Brendan aside. "Brendie," he said. "I have a new one for you today."

"A new what?"

"A new job. More pay and security. Dinzie's place with Jaggers."

"No. There were others who were here before me."

"And who think of this place as another bed, an extra spot to sleep. No. It's yours whether you like it or not."

An hour later, Brendan reported to the Englishman who explained in his crisp accent the various responsibilities of the cabman. "We do a good day's work," he said, "and nobody can complain about us. I've heard only complimentary things about you, Mr. Donnelly. I intend to keep you."

His guard was down. How could he fabricate a dislike for such a straightforward man? He contented himself with regarding England as a place where a few decent men and women resided, as in any place, but where, very likely, the majority was totally alien to the traditions and culture of the Celt. Still, he wished that Jaggers were at least Catholic.

From the start, Jaggers gave Brendan the run of his lorry. Not only did he allow him to take care of it as though it were his own, but he urged him to drive it at every opportunity. "If you don't get behind the wheel," he said, "how are you ever going to get rid of the laborer's bib? It was done for me, the least I can do is pass on the compliment."

On a wet Wednesday morning, Brendan and Jaggers were making deliveries in the center city. As they turned into Bedford Row from Henry Street, they were suddenly faced by a group of Gardai. A barricade stretched from the Lying-in Hospital railings to those of the Georgian houses on the other side of the street.

He became terrified and looked at Jaggers. The Englishman, unperturbed, leaned out the window. He shouted at the nearest Guard. "Hey, mate, what's the bother?"

The tall Guard on the curb did not turn. He simply spoke to nobody in particular when he said, "Boyos. Bomb scare. The road is closed."

"Here?" Jaggers said.

"It's begun, the whole terrible lot of it. Half of the Royal Cinema was made mincemeat of last night. The projectionist is in a bad way at Barrington's Hospital."

"Bloody terrorists! No consideration for the man who has to make a living!" Jaggers's face was red. He spat into the gutter.

Brendan said nothing. He had to admit that the news upset him. Why couldn't the boyos confine their activities to aggravating the Guards and the politicians? What good was it going to do to hurt and inconvenience ordinary people? Were they like a flock of sheep that could be kicked this way and that?

And then, for the first time, it dawned on him. He was outside the movement as a spectator, looking on, as it were, at the paltry show. He had heard nothing of this new phase of bomb threats—he hadn't been to a meeting in a month. Too much work. The time had slipped by, the job and the new friends had engrossed him completely.

He said to Jaggers, "Maybe it's just a scare. The real terrorists are in the North."

"A scare today, Brendie, a bloodbath tomorrow. Don't you remember Hitler's little 'scares'? You were too young."

"But this is Ireland, Brian."

"When madmen look for power, you can expect only madness."

Brendan shifted the gears into idle. "But," he said, "doesn't it take a bit of madness to get those at the top off their arses?"

Jaggers's face clouded. "For what? So that the others can put their arses in the same place? Jesus, Brendan, you haven't swallowed that lie, have you? Is it that they've dressed it up in new clothes, for the young ones who have no memory?"

"What lie?"

"The age-old lie of the revolutionary, the have-not, the reject from society."

"Which is?"

"Which is that all we have now is bad, all that is to come is smashing. I ask of you, have we ever had it so good? There's food on the table, children are being educated, bellies are full."

"But ideas."

"By all means, let's have ideas, but not destructive ones, ones that maim men like the man down at Barrington's, who never raised a hand against anyone."

"But there's corruption . . ."

"Of course there is. Isn't there always? But we have ways and means to oust the culprits the next time we go to the polls. Until then, we have nothing much to fear from them. We know their gait, as it were. They have flaws, but at least they have no murders to their credit. But look at those who would have us believe that they're the saviors of the Republic. Lice. Tinkers. Blackguards. Idlers. The very scum of the earth."

"But what of people like Riordan and McDavitt?"

"Ah, Brendie, the very worst kind. Evil is one thing, but evil with a brain in its head is entirely a different matter altogether. Again, look at Hitler, a mere house painter. Look what we did to a race of good people. I fought the Germans. I sat and ate rations out of a can with them after we dragged them into our base, their guns shattered, their officers dead. They were like ourselves. Cold. Famished. Thinking of a warm fire and a woman beside it and a couple of little children to put their arms about. Human beings. Deceived by words. The words of selfish villains and murderers. God help any honest man who throws in his kit with such filth."

Jaggers's words infuriated him, though he had heard the gist of them many times before. But the man was entitled to his opinion. Of course, it had to be allowed that he was a foreigner, when all was said and done. He chose not to argue. He said, "One thing I know for sure."

"What's that?"

"I wish they'd lift this fucking barricade. We'll sit here all day waiting to deliver the barrels to Shaunessy's."

Chapter 30

Colum did not hear from Riordan for several weeks, and he had begun to feel that the entire affair was a bad joke. However, in late September, he received a registered letter. It contained directions to the Munster Hotel in Kilkenny and also the sum of one hundred pounds advance on salary. He quickly pocketed the envelope and its contents.

Immediately, he set about fabricating an explanation of the move for the family. He had landed a position on the *Kilkenny Herald*. The tip on the job was given to him by one of the masters at Sexton Street, he said. He had not wanted to tell them at the time, but his visit to Kilkenny in July was due in part to this. He had interviewed for the newspaper and the editor had as good as promised him the appointment. He was browned off with teaching, anyway. And this was a marvelous opportunity to take his writing in earnest. When asked if he had given the local papers a try already, Colum quickly brushed the matter aside. Local rags, he called them. Without a shred of professionalism. He wouldn't be caught dead inside their doors.

Before slamming the boot of the car, he stood in the mud of the backyard, a raincoat over his head. He remembered again his first departure, that day long ago when he'd ridden to the train station with his father, afraid that some of his secondary school chums might see him on the shabby donkey and cart. He had been less eager then. Going away to the Brothers. It had only meant an extension of the spiritual rigors practiced at home. The only excitement had been that he would return in the black garb of the Order. But this was the final severance.

When his mother came and put her arms about him, he felt a momentary wrenching of his insides. Perhaps he should tell her the truth, explain all. Instead, he managed a smile. "I'll write," he said.

"It's a pity," she said, "that you won't get to see Brendan before you leave. He talked last night about you stopping over at the Barrel Yard before you left. There's no chance?"

He thought on the coldness that had grown up between himself and his brother over the last few weeks. "Mam," he said, "I'm already a week overdue. I should have packed immediately I got the letter, instead of going around saying good-bye to everybody in the family . . ."

Josie, who was on holiday at the time from the Boot Factory, was less controlled than her mother. After she had kissed him full on the mouth, she took a fit of sobbing and had to be led inside by her mother who returned immediately to say that she would be all right. "Just a fit of nature for you," she said. "God help us."

He drove down the long nettled road, past the railway gates and the stinging smell of the pigs. And he waved to the old fool who stood under the electric standard in College Park and watched with his vacant eyes the eternal circling of the starlings overhead. He crossed O'Dwyer Bridge and turned into the Sandmall. In minutes, he was out on the Dublin Road and free of the city.

Chapter 31

As outlined in the letter, Colum was met at the Munster Hotel by a man named Phil Deegan. Arrangements had been made, Deegan said. Colum would stay at 20 Lelia Place, a tidy residential court in the center city. He would take his meals at home. It was a short drive to the offices of *Cumas*. All was set. The narrow routine excited him. But he was somewhat put off by the fact that Riordan himself had not deemed it important enough to meet him. Tight security. That had to be it, surely.

At the flat, Deegan had a few other instructions. Colum

was never to wear a tie. His license plates were to be changed as soon as possible. He was not to frequent any of the working-class pubs in the city, but, rather, if he had occasion to, take his drinks in one of the many country inns that dotted the suburbs. And in all cases, the rule was to remain as inconspicuous as possible.

When his visitor left, Colum looked out over the city. He thought that he could distinguish the roof of Sheila's flat far off in the distance. But then he realized that he was facing south and not north. He wondered what she might be doing. He looked at his watch. Six o'clock. Perhaps he should call? Instead, he lay back on his bed. He remembered the emphatic note in Deegan's voice as he said, "No contacts with anybody. Absolutely nobody. You'll have to be a bit like a hermit, I'm afraid, so far as the city is concerned."

But there was an intrigue to this, whether real or imagined. So different from the boredom of Sexton Street. He thought back to the Tuesday of the previous week when he had strolled to the upper part of William Street. He had met some of his lads coming out of the school. "Oh, Mr. Donnelly," they said, "are you ever coming back? The master that they've passed us on to is an absolute bore. We read from our books or copy from the board all day long. And he hasn't a bit of a story to tell. He's a musty old codger." They had said, too, that complaints had been made by several parents as to his having been let go. A petition had been signed and . . .

He turned on the small telly and took a cigarette from its pack. It had been the first he had ever bought. The knawn had come on him as he was driving down. But having stopped at a roadside kiosk and purchased the Players, he had no longer felt the urge to smoke. Now he lit the cigarette and put it to his mouth. The smoke tasted dry but nonetheless satisfying.

The *Cumas* offices were situated below a large tire shop on the outskirts of Kilkenny. No indication of their presence

109

could be detected from the road or for that matter from any part of the grounds or shop itself. To gain entrance, it was necessary to park behind the building, unlock one of the rear storeroom doors, descend two flights of stairs, and finally enter by way of another door.

"But the tire shop," Colum asked Deegan. "Is it real or what?"

"Oh, yes. It's run by our own, of course. As a matter of fact, it sold more tires than most other outlets in the city last year."

"You're joking!"

"No."

Before leaving the car, Colum had caught a glimpse of some of the workers. Plainly dressed. Nothing garish. Blues. Grays. Tweeds. And he realized that he would be hard pressed to recognize any of these people again. He looked down at his own sober clothes. A turtleneck. Navy slacks. Black shoes. Deegan had said, "That's the stuff. You'll make the perfect subversive."

As they came through the final doorway, Colum was surprised. In contrast to the drab decor of the upper level, the offices before him were brightly lit and attractively furnished. Each desk was equipped with an electric typewriter, and though the predominant color of the furniture was gray, it nonetheless appeared warm and inviting. The room was cosy. At the far end he noticed a tray which contained a steaming teapot. A dish of biscuits was placed beside it. A plastic radio stood on a bracket above.

The place seemed deserted except for a face that appeared and disappeared behind the glass partitions of one of the cubicles at the back of the room. Finally, it materialized into a tall crew-cut man dressed in a tan shirt and trousers. When he spoke, it was clear that he was American. "Good morning," he said. "I'm Jim Kruger. And you must be Colum."

"Yes." Colum extended his hand.

"I've heard a lot about you. Taig can't say enough."

Kruger leaned against the desk. "I suppose you're surprised to see this place uninhabited. Well, we've just remodeled. Everything's new, brand new. All furnished with American bucks."

"Mr. Riordan mentioned."

"Yes. Anyway, let me explain. I'm here as a training supervisor. Former advertising executive from New York— would you believe it? Now I'm a propagandist! Ha! But as I was saying, I'll be here until yourself and the other office workers begin getting the hang of things."

"Others?"

"Oh, yes. Didn't you know? There'll be three of you in all."

"Mr. Riordan didn't explain fully."

He could not conceal his disappointment. Riordan had promised him the job of editor, not office worker. And no mention had been made of the others. Still, a man had to learn to lead, and when he had learned, there had to be those who were led. He'd bide his time.

Kruger continued. "So," he said, "I'll be working with you for several weeks—as long as it takes for you to learn the ropes."

"I see."

"Did Taig explain the operation?"

"No. Not exactly."

Kruger lit a cigarette. He offered one to Colum, but he waved the pack away. "No, thank you," he said.

"Well, here it is. First of all, our boys call in on one of the lines." He pointed to the three phones on a large desk at the back of the room. "They pass on the info to us—word of police activity, arrests, ambushes, searches, and so forth. We, in turn, make careful note of every nuance, asking questions on weather, amount of light, lay of the land, and whatnot. In reconstructing the story, you see, it is important to mention every detail."

"So that if the reader believes you to be truthful about the insignificant details, he will also give you credit for the main facts."

"Taig was right. You catch on marvelously."

"Thank you."

"Anyway, the rest is easy. We hold a staffing each week when all the stories are gathered, and we decide which we will print and how we will present them."

Colum rubbed his right eye.

"Still a little sleepy?" Kruger said. "You need a cuppa."

"Yes. I'll have a cup."

Kruger walked to the small tray and began pouring the tea. "Sugar?" he asked.

"One spoon."

Colum looked about him at the empty office. He turned to Kruger and said, "Were the old offices here?"

"Yes. Of course we've enlarged quite a bit. A whole new operation now—regional offices of the paper in Munster, Leinster, Connaught, and Ulster. And a separate edition for each province. Almost like *Time,* you might say."

"And the staff of the old *Cumas?*"

"I got rid of them fast. Morons. Little boys playing men's games."

Colum took the cup extended to him. He gulped down the hot tea.

Chapter 32

Brendan moved the sughan chair closer to the fire. Outside, the rain beat down in torrents. It was one of those Saturday mornings when he and Jaggers were off work. He had little to do but sit by the hearth and read Friday night's *Leader.*

"Brendan," his mother said, "is there any chance that

you'd run on in to Bella Daly's for something for me?"

He was a little annoyed at being disturbed, but he said, "Sure, Mam. What is it?"

"Dye."

"What color?"

"Green. I want to dye Josie's skirt, the pink one."

"Okay," he said and reached for his topcoat and hat.

He backed the Morris Minor into the mud and water at the end of the road and then spun the wheel all the way to the left. He cursed under his breath. When were they going to treat the people of Park like ordinary citizens and provide them with proper drainage and sanitation? By God, the next time they had a city council meeting, he'd be there. He'd had enough of this second-class treatment. They were fast enough in getting their share of his few pounds come tax time. Bastards!

As usual, the railway gates were closed against him. But he did not mind too much. He parked the car and stepped into the gate-box. Jimmy Byrnes was seated beside the brazier. "Brendie," he said. "Pull up a seat."

"Thanks."

"The train won't be long."

"Ah, no trouble."

"And how's the job? Lord, you're putting up weight from all that porter. But you're looking tip top."

"We don't drink as much as you give us credit for."

"Go on! Even the rats in that place are stoatered and seeing things half the time, by all accounts. I once heard of a fellow over there who had a pet rat, and the two of them would sit down to supper with a pint of Guinness in front of them . . ."

The roar of the oncoming diesel train drowned out Jimmy's voice. Brendan just laughed to himself. He'd always loved old Jimmy. He was a proper character. Of old stock, the oldest in the parish. He reached out and touched the rosy-faced man. "Jimmy," he said, "your yarns will come back to haunt you."

Brendan got in his car. His mother would have a fit if he dawdled too much longer. And Josie would be without a skirt. He'd never hear the end of that one. He pressed his foot down on the accelerator.

At Priest's Estate, he turned onto the bank. Ahead of him, the mist made the long stretch seem like some unreal country, robbed of any life. The vision gave him a lonely feeling. But he shrugged it off, focusing his eyes for a moment on the stocky figure of a man huddled against Priest's Wall. Nobody he knew. And it would be foolish to offer a ride. These days it was dangerous. Not like long ago.

Having passed the man, Brendan was immediately struck by a sense of uneasiness. Had he known the face? It would never do to leave a friend or relative stranded in the storm. What was it about him that had produced this odd effect? It wasn't his face, he decided. His hat? The coat across his shoulders? The high boots? His red scarf? O Lord Jesus! That was it! Liam Daly's red scarf!

He turned the car into the ditch and jumped from behind the wheel. He ran back through the rain. When he reached the wall, the man, a young fellow not more than twenty-five, stared back at him out of the mist.

Suddenly, Brendan faltered. He remembered the other embarrassing incident on the docks and the look of terror on the poor man's face. What right did he have to go around throttling people? None. His hands fell to his sides.

"Morning," he said.

"Morning."

Brendan shifted his weight. "Ah," he said, "I know this sounds a bit strange, but I stopped because your scarf caught my eye. A friend of mine lost his neckerchief—just like your own, that special red. I was wondering if maybe . . ."

"This scarf?" the man said, fingering the bright material.

"Yes."

"Well, to tell you the truth, sir, it might be his at that."

"What?" Brendan was taken aback by the man's honesty.

"Where did he lose it?"

"He's not sure. Maybe on his way out to our place." He pointed north.

"Then it's probably it."

"Why?"

"I found it here on this bank."

"When was that?"

"Back in May. The last part of May."

"Was it of a Saturday night?"

"No, by God. But you're close. It was early of a Sunday morning. I came out the bank here for a bit of a stroll after Mass and Communion. You know how the Host often leaves a bit of a sour taste in your . . ."

"Yes. I know."

"Well, anyway, that's when I found it."

"Was it on the road or on the wall or what?"

"On the road. In the channel. And it was filthy. It had blood on it."

"Blood?"

"Yes. I thought that it was a bandana thrown away by one of the rugby players from Pa Healy's Field." He pointed to the sports field across the road. "I thought nothing of it."

"I see."

"Is there anything the matter?" the man inquired, catching the paleness in the other's face. "Are you all right?"

"Yes. Just a bit of the black dog."

"Ha!"

Brendan remembered. "Can I give you a lift on into town?" he asked.

"The blessings of God on you, sir. It'll save me a soaking."

They lowered their heads and walked towards the car.

Chapter 33

Colum found his tasks at *Cumas* to be more than exciting. He saw every word bombarded with meanings and extensions and hues. There were nights when he left the newspaper offices as late as midnight and was back again with the pale fall's first sun. He rarely slept more than a few hours. Words were like children to him. They danced, they played, they stepped in and out of shadows, and their moods were dictated by their companions about them. Their faces filled with gloom or joy or pain or indifference. It was a grand game.

And with the life at *Cumas*, he realized more than ever before the dalliance and elusiveness of truth, if, in fact, he wondered, it existed at all, if perhaps it were all a dream, this solitary existence on the planet, a gorgeous nightmare in some mad god's festered brain. First of all, the "facts" were reported over the telephone, sometimes by participants in the raids or ambushes, other times by informers within the Gardai. Then, this hard news was filtered, softened, put in suitable contexts and perspectives, ballooned—God knew what!—and presto! It came out on the glossy sheets of *Cumas* as a reality in its own right. There, there on the page, symbols standing for other symbols that were communicated through other symbols that were representations of further symbols that stood for images. Jesus! the maze of it. And he felt no real conspiracy in his work, no true tampering, because all about him existed the very exact duplicates of his performance. *The Press, The Independent, The Times*—they too were coloring, arranging, making the truth more palatable. And the national news service, RTE, the same. It was life! He doubted that if he were actually present at the events, he doubted that even then would he have experienced what had fully taken place, or even if it mattered in the long run.

His dedication did not go unnoticed by Kruger. On one occasion, when they were working alone in the office, he turned to Colum and said, "You're ahead of them all, Colum. They'll never catch you."

"Who?"

"The other men here. Oh, they're good, and they've learned fast. But they don't have your experience, your power to become part and parcel of the maelstrom of words. You're the best there is."

"Thank you."

"As a matter of fact, I have yourself in mind to run this shop when I leave for Dublin next week. The experience at the helm will do you good. You'll have no bother."

"But the others?"

"They're just like schoolboys. They see that you're different. You're their idol, believe me."

Riordan himself echoed Kruger's praise on those rare occasions when he arrived to occupy his cubicle at the rear. Colum often wondered what transpired between himself and Kruger in those highly secretive meetings held behind the drawn curtains. Did they talk of the newspaper itself? Of him? Or the vast network of I.R.A. contacts throughout the country? Of the latest caper pulled? (He often felt a twinge of envy for the men in the field. But he told himself that his job was much more important. It was he who put the last heroic coating on, so to speak.) Or was the conversation on a higher plane? Did they speak in familiar terms of international revolutionaries, call them by their first names? Often he felt irritated by his exclusion as though he were only half-important. But perhaps he would soon be part of that inner sanctum. His flesh crawled at the prospect of such confidences and heady responsibility. Yet he might have to wait for several years. He knew that Kruger was more than just a training supervisor.

Chapter 34

Brendan sat in his room and watched the moon rise over Mount Keeper. It was bright enough for him to see quite a distance across the fields. Before him were a few pencils and sheets of paper on which he had drawn several diagrams and listed as many names. He knew that somewhere in the maze of roads, boreens, and open spaces between his house and the Canal Bank lay a clue to the events that had taken place the night when Liam Daly was drawn to his death. But too much time had gone by. Even if he examined every ounce of earth between here and there, he still would come up with nothing that the naked eye could discern as evidence. But every animal left its smell. And the killers of his friend would be no exception to the rule (he reasoned that to move the body, dead or alive, from the spot near Priest's Estate, had taken the efforts of more than one man). But who were they?

Brendan poured himself a cup of tea. Somewhere before those remaining hours there was a clue. If only he could put his finger on it. He went back again to the beginning. First of all, Liam had spoken of the ambush, at Conway's pub in Sandmall. But, of course, there was no way of knowing if this incident had been his downfall. He could have spoken again of this stupid caper. Others could have heard him. But who? Who had felt insecure enough to do away with the misfortune? And Riordan had assured him that the organization had not been officially involved. It had to be as he had concluded in the last hours—the work of some obscure hotheads, eager to win favor within the movement. It had been done before; it could be the same again. It *had* to be.

Perhaps he should take his evidence to Riordan, he thought. But he decided against this. It was his affair alone. And Riordan hadn't cared two hoots for Liam's death . . .

Conway's pub was packed, and he had difficulty finding a

stool at the counter. When he did, it was just in time to catch Angela as she skimmed a pint with a wooden ruler and asked, "Who else is ready?" Several voices spoke up, but she handed the drink to Brendan. "You deserve it," she said. "You're the man that saw to it that I had porter during the work slow-up. The blessings of God on you, Brendie."

"Your health," he said and sucked down the black liquid.

After about half an hour, the pub began to clear, and Angela wiped her face on her spotless bib. She sat down on a little cushioned stool, below Brendan's place at the bar. "Oh," she said, "these rugby games will be the death of me."

"Who won?"

"I thought you were a parish man?"

"I am."

"And you don't know who won?"

"I haven't been following . . ."

"Shannon, of course."

He waited for several minutes before asking her his question. Then he said, "Angela, I hate to be harping back to that day this year when Liam died, but it's still bothering my mind."

"Ah, sure," she said, "it was a great blow to you."

"Well, what I'm getting at is this. Remember that day when he was here and he shouted about the man who ambushed Mulcahy having relatives in the parish?"

"I recall it well."

"The thing is this—and I know I've asked you before—were there any of the boyos here? I know that you know a few of them." He lowered his voice. "Including myself," he added.

She smiled. "No," she said. "Just Mick Feeney, the cabman. Arch Naughton. And Kuck Lynch. None of them are in the movement. They're too old. They're not like that, either." Her voice had shades of bitterness in it.

"No one else?"

"No one."

The man on the next stool was Gilla Frawley. At her last

words he spoke up. "Ah, there's where you're wrong, Angela Conway," he said. "Wrong as night."

"Don't listen to him at all, Brendan," she said. "I remember as clearly as if it were in front of my eyes."

"Oh, you do now?" said Frawley. He winked at Brendan. "Mind you," he said, "her old brain has been going off this past few years. It's addled with the thoughts of business and business and more business."

She made a swipe at the impish man with her towel. "We won't mention the condition of your brains . . ."

"As sharp as a pin this very minute," he said. "Think, Angela. Think back."

"Think back to what?"

"Think about the fact that I was here that very day. I came in right at the tail end of the argument. The three lads were sitting over there talking about young Daly's temper."

"So you came in," she said. "What does that make you, the banshee?"

"No. But it makes me the man who climbed the back wall, and the man who passed a tweedy fellow on his way out by the jakes. *Da bhri sin,* as the man says, he must have been in here at the time. Now put that in your pipe and smoke it."

Angela looked at Brendan. She bit her lip. "Brendan," she said, "he's right, though I hate to admit it. I remember now. I'd forgotten about the townie with the tweed cap."

"Who was he?"

"A traveler, I think. He comes in and out of here about once a month. I can't think of his name."

"Try, Angela!"

She faced down the bar. "Raef," she said, "what's that fellow's name that was talking to you over in the corner a few mornings ago? Wears a tweed cap. Has a gold tooth in the front."

"Brosnahan," the call came back. "Jack Brosnahan."

"What does he do? Where does he live?"

"He sells biscuits. Lives up on Bowman Street. Off Wolfe

Tone Street. It's just right there on the corner. Right across from the 'Nook' chip shop. I gave him a lift home once when he was stoatered . . ."

"There you are, Brendie," she said. "There isn't another thing to tell you."

"Thanks," he said. "And give Gilla here two pints and a Paddy on me."

"He's had enough," she said.

"No. He deserves it."

Once outside, he faced in the direction of home. No madness this time. He was going to take it easy. Very slow and easy.

Chapter 35

Kruger was as good as his word. When he left for Dublin the following week, the full responsibility of the office fell to Colum. He had looked forward to this day. It was his first important chance.

However, the office seemed to run itself. The other workers, Cleary and Mangan, were in every way subordinate and came to him on several occasions to seek his advice. He felt that their inquiries were genuine and he affected a casual attitude in each situation. As a result, when Thursday's staffing arrived, both younger men were open and relaxed. He knew that it was essential to dispel their natural apprehension of him. He did not wish to be regarded as a "Johnny-come-lately."

On the afternoon of the staffing, he took Kruger's seat at the mouth of the horseshoe shaped desk and glanced over his own stories for the week. Usual fare, he thought to himself. A man beaten by the Guards in New Ross. Four men arrested for distributing leaflets in Waterford. A bomb scare in Cashel. He polished a phrase here and there and waited for the others to arrange their papers.

Finally, they were ready. "Well, lads," he said. "I'll try to keep it short. You know the routine. The important stories first, the small ones later. Cleary?"

The young Tipperary man looked up from his notes. "Something entirely new," he said.

"What is it?"

"Well, as you know, here in the South we have nothing like what they have up North—pub bombings, slaughter on the streets, out-and-out murder . . ."

"Go on. Get to the point."

"Well, this is different. This is a direct inheritance from Belfast."

"Murder of our own?"

"No. No. A women's march for peace—*in the South!* Catholics and Protestants together. Galway and Limerick last week. How do we handle it?"

"Certainly not in the same manner as the North handles it." He remembered reading an account of the threats leveled against the participants in such a march held in Antrim. "Let me see the story."

Cleary handed him the sheaf of papers. Pinned to the top right hand corner were photographs of the previous Sunday's march. He looked closely at the faces of his fellow citizens. His heart jumped when he thought that he recognized one here or there. But he was mistaken. There was too much shadow, probably caused by the bad light. He glanced at the words beneath. Cold. Rain. Skies heavily overcast. Flooding on the streets . . .

Cleary and Mangan were waiting. It was up to him to make the move. "Well," he said (he hoped that his voice did not waver), "I see it this way. The North has its methods, and we have ours. Their goal is complete disintegration and then rebirth. Ours is different. Here in the South, the majority of the people have nationalistic leanings, though I will admit that they are at a low ebb at present. Our business is not one of destruction and then resurrection. It is one of *injection*, injection of the old nationalism into the new apathy. Certainly we must agitate a bit, but not to any extreme degree."

The two subordinates were looking at him closely. They knew that he had only arrived a few days before themselves, but there was a fever about him that they seemed to lack. Perhaps it was his association with Riordan and Kruger, they didn't rightly know.

He continued with power now. "So," he said, "my decision is to praise the women's march, say that we are behind it, that we are for peace as much as the next man, but that the fault lies with the Government, which has lost its respect and dignity and its ability to deal with the butchers in Westminister. The women are the people—and when was the I.R.A. *not* behind the people of this country who ask only peace and quiet and the opportunity to raise decent families?" The perspiration shone on his forehead.

"Yes," Cleary said, "but won't they see that we're the ones behind the bomb scares and . . ."

"No one has really been hurt as yet. If someone has; then he has been a foreigner. Few of our own have received more than a scratch. If we begin to condemn our own, we'll be writing our death warrant."

"So we must confuse the issue as much as possible for the time being?"

"Right—until we see where this women's thing is going. It may be just a fad. It may die out in a month. But until we know, we have to take it handy."

"You're right."

The others shuffled their papers. He breathed easily again. For a moment he thought that he had lost their confidence. But he had held the day. He had been decisive and clearsighted. If only they knew . . .

Chapter 36

B rendan Donnelly had little difficulty in finding the stucco house where Brosnahan lived. It was directly opposite the Nook chip shop as the man at the pub had said. He crossed the narrow lane called Bowman Street.

He raised the heavy knocker and allowed the metal to pound with a heavy rhythm on the brass plate. He could hear the sound echo throughout the house.

Almost immediately, the door was opened by a diminutive woman in a red bib. "Are you mad?" she cried. "Are you trying to knock the house down? Who are you? Jack-in-the-beanstalk?"

"My name is Brendan Donnelly," he said sharply. "I'm looking for your husband."

The woman saw his stern expression. "Well, boy," she said, softly now, "I'm afraid you'll have a long look. He's been buried up in Mount St. Lawrence this many a year."

"You're not Mrs. Brosnahan?"

"O Lord, no. Save me from that."

"Why?"

"The man's a blackguard . . ."

"Where is he now?"

"He's off."

"Off where?"

"On his holidays. He goes this time every year."

"Where?"

"London. Over in England."

"I know. When will he be back?"

"A month. The longer he stays away the better. A woman doesn't need lodgers like him. If it wasn't for the money . . ."

"Why?"

"Because his kind bring bad luck to decent people. Drink. Women. Cards . . ."

"Thank you very much," he said as he touched his hat and stepped backwards into the street.

He left the tangle of tenements and run-down buildings by climbing Barrack Hill and taking the street that ran past the Technical Institute. And at last he was out in the open again.

Chapter 37

Colum delivered the portfolio of stories to the print shop and distributing office in Cuffe's Grange, a small town south of Kilkenny, and went straight home. He was exhausted. It had been a long day. He felt the muscles of his chest and left arm tighten in stress. What if he had made the wrong decision on the women marchers? What would Riordan say? Do? Would it be the end of the job? Would he return home again in a different kind of shame? He tormented himself with the possibilities.

He had not eaten supper, as had been the case on many other nights, but this time he felt too exhausted to drive to one of the outlying roadhouses for a sandwich and a drink. He thought of Sheila. He bet that she'd be glad to see him. She'd surely insist on offering him food if he dropped by. And lovemaking. But he remembered Deegan's words from the beginning. No mixing whatsoever. He couldn't afford a slip. Not now, especially. He was tired, anyway, he told himself. A good night's rest would be just the ticket.

As he opened the hall door to his flat, he saw the white envelope on the floor. He stooped to pick it up. It was from Josie. Since he had left home, she had written faithfully every week, never missing a Thursday. He had come to look forward to her gossipy letters and had been as regular himself in responding.

He leaned back in his wooden chair and switched on the electric fire. He read the letter slowly. His mother had a cold but was getting over it. Seoirse had been promoted to manager of the sweet shop where he worked. (Colum suspected that the boss had done so as a precaution against having his profits devoured by the fat counterman.) Brendan was still at the Guinness yard and working overtime almost every night. There had been several bomb scares in the city. The whole town was up in arms. The Men's Confraternity at the Redemptorists' was going to march down O'Connell Street on Sunday morning in protest of the turmoil. She was worried if he were taking good care of himself. And Ellen Sullivan had asked to be remembered to him.

He reread her letter. He was not in the mood to write, but if he put it off, he might not get a minute to himself until the weekend. He uncovered the Adler that he had borrowed from the *Cumas* office.

He considered his letters to his sister to be an outlet for the kind of writing to which he had recently become unaccustomed. Of course, he was obliged to omit certain facts about the office and his particular role, but he felt that he relentlessly tried to strip his words of unnecessary colorations. Things were going well, here, he said. He was loving his job. He had poor chance to go out at night and when he did it was only to have a few pints with his young associates, Cleary and Mangan. (He rarely had more than two as the conversations of the men left him cold.) No. He was a regular monk, he said, and laughed at himself as he typed the words. Too bad the Brothers didn't copy manuscripts as they did in ancient Ireland—he might have found a niche then.

He closed his letter by saying that he would surely find the time soon to make his first visit home. Before sealing the envelope, he enclosed three of the blue bills from the several in his wallet. However, in hesitation, he withdrew one of these. A person could never know; he might need the extra bit of cash. The car might need repairs . . .

He had made no mention of Brendan in his letter. And this was usual. He had not forgiven him for that day near the Shannon Fields. The cheek of that uneducated oaf to lay hands on him like that. Just like his father—a peasant exerting his stupid animal strength. He cringed at the recalled humiliation.

He looked at his watch. Nearly eleven o'clock. He'd catch

the half-eleven post if he hurried. The postbox was only eight or nine blocks down the street. He put the envelope under his gabardine to shield it against the rain.

Chapter 38

When Colum reported to work on Monday, he found the *Sunday Independent* on his desk. A glance to his rear certified that Riordan was in his office (he could see the faint glow of the light through the thick fibers of the curtains). Meeting with Kruger, no doubt, he thought. He opened the newspaper.

Suddenly the blood surged to his face. He dropped the paper onto the desk and looked again at the headlines:

TWO WOMEN BEATEN IN PEACE MARCH

ONE IN CRITICAL CONDITION IN

WEXFORD HOSPITAL

What did it mean? That *he* was at fault? They were strangers—Wexford—the other side of the country, but, nonetheless, his territory. What effect had his words had on them? Had his editorial encouraged their actions? Had they taken heart in his words and walked into the danger? (Did he have *that* much influence?) Or was the action a retaliation by the rank and file against his stand? Was this a scorning of his position? Surely it was Riordan who had left the newspaper. Somehow he felt that he had really botched it. The job was gone. He began to dread the look on Riordan's face.

He heard the door behind him open and the footsteps begin in his direction. One. Two. Three. Four. Five. Six. He turned slowly to face his accuser.

He looked up into Riordan's face. To his surprise, the man was smiling and saying, "Colum, so good to see you. How did everything go?"

Colum bit his upper lip. "Well," he said, "I'm not so sure . . ."

Riordan laughed. "Don't be modest," he said. "Sure you're sure."

"What?" Colum's heart was pounding.

Riordan pointed to the newspaper. "Unfortunate," he said, "but they asked for it in a way. Wexford is a bastion of strong revolutionary feelings. They were taking their lives in their hands."

"One woman is critical . . ."

"That is life, Colum. You had nothing to do with it. You praised the women's efforts. Wasn't that your stand?"

"Yes," he said weakly.

"I read your editorial on the way back from Dublin. Who told you, by the way, to take this viewpoint?"

"I told myself. But . . ."

"And you think that I'm vexed at you over it?"

"Yes."

Riordan burst into laughter. "Nothing could be further from the truth," he said. "You've learned well. You've gauged the mood of the people in the South. Three months ago, who would have heard of the likes of women's marches, until those two bitches, Corrigan and Williams, got the notion? Nobody in his or her proper mind. But there it is, as real as day, now, and we must deal with it. Ireland is a dancing floor, Colum, dancing as well as being something that is danced upon. The South will not abide too much violence—it's had peace for so long, whereas in the North it's a way of life. And we must use this pacifism to our benefit, unless we wish to lose all base and have North *and* South down our throats. If that ever happens, we'll be run into the sea like snakes. We must praise this pacifism, for the time being. We must seem to align ourselves with its goals and condemn terrorism as alien to the Irish way, the Irish vision for the future." His voice had gained a rhapsodic quality and his eyes were raised.

"There's no fear of getting lost in the jumble?"

"No, not at all. We will know exactly what is going on—

always. We will know that the man who has been a terrorist and a bully and now reveals himself as a man of peace is far more attractive than the weakling who followed the rule all his life—the Prodigal Son, for example. That old blind whore, De Valera, was like a god in this country for half a century and he nothing more than a twerp to start off. Patrick Pearse the same. All of them. It's a fact of human nature. But the confusion and frustration must be kept warm. There must be on one end the threat of violence and on the other the mire of vacillation."

"So it's a setup in which only a few know the truth?"

"Exactly—the elite. You made a fine move for us. I was in Dublin because of the marches. But I had no need to tell you our decision. You double-guessed us."

"So you will appear to want peace on the surface and yet beneath it all you will agitate to make those in the Dail look powerless to stem the tide of disruption?"

"And all the while the eejits out there will be struggling to figure out who's a Provo and who's a regular, who's a terrorist and who's a man of peace at heart. The I.R.A. will be all things to all men. The others won't be given a thought."

Riordan smiled, and Colum noticed his upper teeth scrape his lower lip. "And Wexford? you ask. I agree—some go too far. Of course, it's hard to contain the lads who have been up North or in the internment camps. The complacency all about turns them into mad dogs, at times. And this period of transition will not go down well with them. Alas, they do not have our qualities of mind." He touched Colum on the shoulder.

Riordan continued, "Not to change the subject, but there's excellent news. Kruger is gone for good. Back to New York. You're now the editor of this newspaper. Run it as you wish and will. It takes an Irishman to run an Irish job. Fuck those Yanks."

"What?"

"You're the boss. We'll have a new man to replace you at the desk in a few weeks. A young fellow like yourself. Teacher, too. From Kerry. Listowel. Sean Keane. You'll train him as Kruger trained you. He's like yourself, very bright. You'll both get on like wildfire."

Colum was astonished. He had imagined being eventually free of Kruger's authority, but he had no notion that *he* would be appointed in the American's place. He stuttered. "When . . ."

"Right away. This minute. A new rank. A new salary. Congratulations, and more power to you!" Riordan's hand was extended, and Colum took it. The old man then turned and walked towards his office. "If there's anything that comes up this morning," he said, "go ahead and handle it. I'll be very busy."

"Right."

As Riordan closed the door behind him, Colum remembered that he'd had another question on the Wexford incident. But he did not speak. What was he, a child that flinched at the first pain? So two people were given a hiding? What was new about that? Violence had always been the native pastime. Walk down any street and what did you see? Youngsters with scabs on their faces beating the daylights out of their companions on the pretext of a dobber stolen or a pickie slate kicked in the wrong direction. And on every corner in the town, the scarred faces of tinkers, begging for the price of another bottle so that reality might be obscured before the opening of the next fresh skull. And the new brutality—muggings, false arrests, trial without jury, break-ins, interrogations. Everybody was at it, and the I.R.A.'s contribution, though it received the most publicity, was only a speck in the eye by comparison. Was he making a cod of himself thinking that in some way he might be kept free of it all? He was no longer in the monastery. He should be glad that he was on the side of power and that those who were being chastised were strangers.

He dismissed his scruples. What success! And so soon. He wished that he could write and throw it in the face of Brother Roland. Or in Brendan's face.

As he moved the typewriter and files to Kruger's former office, he had only one nagging consideration. Why hadn't

Riordan chosen to declare himself in the darkened private office? If he, Colum, were equal to Kruger, why was he not allowed the same privileges? What in heaven was so special about the bloody office, anyway?

Chapter 39

Brendan returned late from work on a dreary Monday night. He had stopped off with Jaggers and several others of the men to have a few pints at Mick Quilligan's.

As he lifted the latch, he imagined his mother and Josie waiting inside, ready to give out to him for his lateness. Supper burnt on the hob. The bread cold. The tea stewed . . .

The kitchen was empty. He hung his coat and hat up on a nail and walked into the hallway. He followed the murmur of voices to Josie's room and knocked on the door. "Come in," he heard his mother say.

A fire was lit in the grate. His mother sat to the left of the mantel. Josie was sitting up in bed, a cup of hot milk in her hands. "What's up?" he said.

"It's herself," the mother answered. "If I told her once, I told her a thousand times. She's working too hard. Running herself down . . ."

"It's nothing," Josie said. "I had a bit of a pain in my right side at work. I came home early, that's all. I'll be all right tomorrow."

Brendan stared at her. "Listen," he said, "why don't you let me run you on in to Barrington's? It wouldn't take a minute. You could have one of the doctors look at you. There'd be no harm in it."

"Oh, Jesus, save us!" Josie said and laughed. "Since when did you become so lovable? Now he's concerned about my health and welfare . . ."

"Will you shut up!" he said with embarrassment. "If you

want to go in, I'll take you in. If you don't, then don't make a mockery of me."

Josie did not speak for several seconds. When she did, her tone had changed. "All right," she said. "I'm sorry to make a scoff. But I'll be okay. There's no need. If it isn't gone by the morning, I'll be after you for a lift."

"Okay," he said. "It'll be no bother. If we can't do it for our own, who else is there?"

He left the room and entered the kitchen. He took a seat by the hearth. Women! You couldn't be nice to them, he thought. He was glad he wasn't married. Still, Brian Jaggers had no complaints. The Englishman spoke of his wife constantly. But he supposed that if you found the right one, one that wasn't a carper . . . Josie was all right. Her fault was that her father had put her on a pedestal. How he used to hold her on his lap and sing silly songs in all kinds of different voices. Poor Seoirse Hayes. He'd have his work cut out for him, the creature.

He picked up the *Leader* and read the headlines:

MAYOR OF PORTLAOISE HOLDS

COUNCIL MEETING

THEN REVEALS MURDER OF HIS WIFE

HOMES OF OLD AGE PENSIONERS VANDALIZED

BY YOUTHS

He wondered if they made the bloody news up! And as for what was reported in *Cumas*, he couldn't make head nor tail to that. The weekly paper had gone from printing the words of all the old traditional songs, even given up on the stories of the Red Branch. It was like an American magazine—all philosophy and politics and talk. Rubbish!

He folded the *Leader*, and, thinking better of throwing it into the flames, he placed it in the small wicker basket by the hob. Perhaps his mother or Josie had not had a chance to read it yet. Whatever there was to read, God knows!

Chapter 40

S ean Keane arrived on a Friday afternoon, and he was
introduced to Colum by Riordan. "Here he is," the old
man said, "the honest pride of Listowel."

Colum extended his hand. "Delighted to meet you," he
said.

"Delighted to meet *you*," Keane replied. "I've read everything you've written. When will we be seeing some more—
under your name, that is?"

"Soon. Soon." They laughed together.

Colum looked at Keane as Riordan was introducing the
young lad to Cleary and Mangan. The fair complexion. The
sandy hair. The blue eyes. The scampish smile and hearty
laugh. He had somehow known that he would like him the
moment he had lowered his head to come through the
doorway.

Later in the afternoon, when the first stories of the new
week had trickled in and the phones were quiet, for once,
Colum turned to Keane, who was intently studying the small
manual of phrases and word arrangements compiled by
Colum himself.

"This categorization is ingenious," Keane was saying.
"There's a twist of language here to suit every occasion."

"Thank you."

"*You* made it up?"

"Yes."

"Go on! It's a complete system. You ought to sell it to all
the other subversive groups in the world. It'd sell like hot
cakes."

"I might, yet."

"Include me when you do. I'll be your P.R. man."

"It's a bargain."

Keane returned to the pages before him. And it was some
time before he put the manual down and said, "Say, is there
any chance we could go out for a pint? I'm as thirsty as a
sewer worker."

"Well, we could drive out into the country," Colum answered. "There's a nice little pub in Tullaroan. But there'd be no need to even go there, in this weather." He pointed to the snow falling steadily outside the skylight. "We could stop by a shop in town and pick up a few jars. And I've got some sausages at home in the fridge . . ."

"Colum, I don't want to be a beggar. I . . ."

"Will you stop! I welcome the company. I haven't had a visitor since I came here."

"Well . . ."

"It's settled, then. Put away that magic book of mine and let's go."

"What about Riordan?"

"He'll be in that bloody dark office until midnight."

"Oh, all right."

The flat was cold and Colum turned on the electric fire. Still, the heat was not sufficient to warm them. "I'd put in a bit of fire, Sean," he said, "but to tell you the truth, I haven't been able to get one started. They all go out. The newspaper won't take."

"That's because it's *Cumas*." Sean laughed. "Here, let me try my hand. I've lit many a fire, I tell you—and not all of them were in grates!"

Colum pondered Keane's first remark as he handed him the bundle of sticks. How had he meant it? Was it that the paper was immune to destruction? Or was it that it was dead and without the energy to flame out? No matter how he looked at it, the comment seemed to contain a note of scorn. Still, he reminded himself, Keane was an excellent writer (Riordan had passed on samples of the boy's work) and his jokes should have nothing to do with his capabilities. He himself had no patriotic notions, and yet he was an expert in his work. He had put the quandary from his mind when he said, "I'll start the sausages."

"And don't forget that jar of porter!"

"No. No." Colum laughed at the other's distended tongue and popping eyes. He thought that he was beginning to understand the lad, after all—he was a proper character.

Later, when they had finished several pints of stout, and sat now between the blaze of the fire and the dull red glow of the electric heater, Sean Keane said, "So, Colum, how long did you spend away in the Brothers?—Riordan was telling me."

"About five years."

"They must have grabbed you out of short pants?"

"Almost. I wanted to go, though. Of course, I would rather have gone in the priests. But they laughed at me. They said, get an education first and we'll talk to you."

"What priests?"

"Cistercian."

"What? Locked away down in Mount Melleray, digging a foot of your own grave each day, getting up at all hours of the night to kneel prostrate before the tabernacle . . ."

"Yes. They even invited me there for a week."

"Did you go?"

"I did. Sometimes, I wish that they had allowed me to stay."

He thought with nostalgia of that Saturday long ago when he had arrived at Mount Melleray. How he had wandered silently into the clerestory of the great church. How he had knelt spellbound before the altar. He remembered looking up at the throng of priestly monks as they raised their voices in chant. And their ceremony had reached out, it seemed, to envelop him into their sacredness. Oh, the majestic words. The sapphired monstrance. The strange call of the incense. The humeral veil. O Lord, he knew that this would have been enough, if only they had accepted him, made him a priest of God, capable of anointing the dying, handling the Eucharist, and permitting his young priest's voice to soar thunderously above the half-light of the cathedral, calling out Christ's compassion on all those below—"Verily, do I say unto thee, this day thou shalt be with me in Paradise." Or the face contorted, enunciating the condemnation of the ages— "Depart from me, you cursed . . ." Instead, he had entered the Brothers. And they had offered him so little against the temptations of the world and the draw of the agnostic grayness—a black suit and a half collar. No wonder he had fallen by the wayside. A man needed all the power of the trimmings, their magic . . .

"Well," Sean was saying, "I never had a vocation to anything—girls, maybe." He laughed boyishly.

"Not the writing?"

"No. That's second nature. John B. Pratt was my uncle."

"You're joking!"

"No."

"Oh, I used to love his plays. But I haven't been to a playhouse since I left Limerick."

"Oh, John B. is a card. He says that he took up writing one night after seeing a Shakespeare play. Says that he saw every one of the characters from the play on the streets of Listowel. All he had to do was invite them to supper and get them to talking. Now he meets with them every week. And, of course, his yarns come out of that."

"He's pulling your leg."

"I don't know, really."

"But yourself. Haven't you done any fiction? Poetry? I read your articles, they were perfect. We're lucky to have you."

"No fiction or poetry, unfortunately. I don't have the mind for it. I'm just an essayist, at best. I was given only one half of the cake—the reality side. Fiction and poetry are out of my class. They're for the likes of yourself."

"But you can try. The work here will draw you in. Wait and see . . ."

"No. I've read your stuff in the Dublin papers. You're going places. I'm not. I suppose you have a novel or two done by now . . ."

"Well . . ." Colum put his glass to his mouth and gulped the black liquid.

"I'll never forget the story about the girl with the coarse and crusted hands and how she kept them covered all the time."

"In case she'd infect the rest of her body."

"Right."

"I've forgotten much of it, to tell the truth."

"The irony was powerful—the rest of her body was what was really infected, not her poor naturally rough hands."

"It was a bit romantic, I'm afraid. It was a very early story . . ."

"Oh, no. It got to the heart of the matter. It was well done."

"Thank you." He paused. "So tell me," he said, "how did you ever come to *Cumas?*"

"Oh, I did a little column for the newspaper in Tralee, something like John B. does in the *Limerick Leader*. Of course, I added a bit of cynicism now and then to get the county council off its arse. The writing came to Riordan's attention— he's a friend of one of my uncles, an I.R.A. man since the time of the Troubles. I saw the opportunity as a grand chance to end the general staleness of my life, to do some serious journalism, and to avail myself of the fantastic salary."

"No patriotism?"

"No. Not much. I'm an honest realist.

"What about the teaching?"

"I got the sack for putting my hands in the knickers of the headmaster's daughter—lovely fat and rosy Mary Cuddahy, God bless her bovine breasts and haunches. Yourself? What was your situation?"

"My students faded away. *Ergo*, I was out of a job."

"Jesus! Life is a hobnail bed, sometimes, isn't it?"

"It is."

Colum poured the contents of the last stout bottle into Sean's glass. He should have bought more stout. He hated to be ever caught out like this.

Chapter 41

Trom the shelter of an alleyway, he watched his man leave the lodging house. Brosnahan was in his fifties, Brendan guessed. Gaudily dressed, with a tweed cap set cockily on his head. He walked with an effeminate air and occasionally stopped before a darkened shop window to smooth back his hair or press his cap more firmly on his crown.

Brendan followed him at a safe distance for several blocks, and when the man was about to enter Joseph's Street, he made his move. From about six feet away, he shouted, "Mr. Brosnahan! Mr. Brosnahan, the informer!"

Brosnahan stopped dead. He turned slowly to face his accuser.

"Mr. Brosnahan, the informer!"

Brosnahan looked up and down the street. "Please stop," he begged. "The walls have ears. What is it you want? Money?" He reached for his wallet.

"Keep your Judas money—the money you got six months ago for turning a man in." Brosnahan's terror had convinced him that this was his man.

"Who are you talking about?"

"You know who I'm talking about. Liam Daly."

"The lad who committed suicide?"

"Suicide my arse! Murder!"

"By the Guards?"

"The Guards?" Brendan was confused for a moment. But then he realized the implication of Brosnahan's admission. "So," he cried, "it was you who gave the information to William Street Barracks? It was you who caused the arrests?"

"But I thought no harm was done. The lads were released. I mean . . ."

"Oh, it's all coming to me now. Liam Daly wasn't arrested because your friends the Guards were waiting to see what he'd do or say next to incriminate the others. And I wasn't grabbed because of an oversight . . ."

138

Brosnahan's voice wavered. "You're a boyo?" he cried. "One of the best."

"But you don't understand," Brosnahan was saying. "I gave your lads the tip, too. He was running at the mouth, saying that he knew who pulled the caper at Annacotty . . ."

"You told someone in the movement as well?"

"Yes," Brosnahan said with desperation. "Sheridan."

"Garoid Sheridan?"

"Yes."

Brendan recognized the name as that of one of the organization principals in the city. The word would have gone from him directly to Riordan. "When did you tell him?" he asked, the words dropping slowly from his lips.

"That Sunday morning."

"*Sunday* morning?"

"That's right."

"But Liam Daly was dead then . . ."

"I know. The information was useless. But he paid me anyway." His head was lowered. "He said that I did good work."

"He paid you anyway?"

"A fiver."

Brendan looked sadly at the frightened pock-faced man. He felt no desire to brutalize him. The word would get out on Brosnahan, sooner or later. And his life wouldn't be worth a trawneen. He stepped silently into the darkness, leaving the man under the weak light of the street lamp.

Chapter 42

The light on Colum's desk had flashed several times before he noticed it. He had been concentrating on the injection of a delicately sour note into the report of a

Franciscan preacher who had come out against the movement, calling it a "den of Communists and agitators." The
clergy had to be handled with kid gloves, despite the fact that
their churches were empty. There were still those who, in
their apostasy, believed that to meddle with the Church
brought on some ancient curse. He dropped the sheets in
front of him and returned to Riordan's office.

He knocked on the heavy paneled door. He heard Riordan
undo the lock. Perhaps this time he would be allowed inside.
However, the old man appeared and beckoned him to one of
the empty cubicles.

When the door was closed and they were seated, Riordan
smiled. "Colum," he said, "I have a little present for you
today. I know that you have been working hard, polishing
the polished, as it were. But this is a bit of the rough
diamond—none of the others have seen it. No distance at all
involved. But perhaps you don't wish to descend to the lower
regions, now that you are master here . . ."

Colum did not enjoy being taunted. "What is it?" he
asked, betraying the slightest annoyance.

"Think back," Riordan said. "Think back to a night in
early July. Remember a dance at Pallas Green. A girl from
Kilkenny, here."

"Listen," Colum said firmly, "I have never visited her, I
have no truck with her or any other woman . . ."

"Oh, don't take me wrong. I know that you have put aside
pleasure, the fleshy . . ."

"But how did you know about her?"

"I'm sorry, Colum. We had to take every precaution
before asking you on. You understand."

He did not respond for several seconds. Then he said, "I
suppose you knew about the arrest?"

"Yes. And it's that that I have the best news on."

"I'd rather forget it."

Colum remembered with bitterness the blur of Guards'
faces and the bellowed command to get out of the car. He

had not forgotten the putrid smells of the cell or the ignominy of having been thrown in among the low life of the city.

"Oh, no, Colum. This is your chance for a discreet revenge."

"What?"

Riordan handed Colum a manila folder. He then stood up from the desk. "Say what you please," he said. "You know that you're your own man here. I just thought that you might wish to kill two birds with the one stone." With that he left the room.

Colum opened the folder. The opening section was typed. It read:

> Michael Keough, arrested by Gardai, night of
> November 28. Taken from Dola to Caherconlish for
> interrogation. Charges: possession of explosives.
> Keough, with organization only one year, gave, under
> pressure, names of several operatives in West
> Limerick area. Four arrests made within last two days.

This was followed by other paragraphs which explained in detail the circumstances surrounding Keough's incarceration and the arrests of the other men. Colum skipped the routine details. Instead, his attention was drawn to Riordan's postscript, written in red ink:

> The Guard in charge of interrogation was one
> Sergeant Michael Flannigan of West Clare. This man, in
> recent months, has made it his personal priority
> to harass our people in the Dola-Caherconlish area.

> This Garda's previous assignment was Killaloe. He spent
> two years there. During that time, he was trainer
> for the local girls' swimming and hockey teams.
> However, in June of this year, he was abruptly
> transferred to Dola, an obscure post. It should be noted
> that Guard Flannigan is not married and was
> often seen in private company with some of his girl
> athletes.

Colum, this was the man who signed you in at
William Street Barracks. Incidentally, he was out of his
jurisdiction in the urban area.

The perspiration stood out on Colum's forehead. He
closed his eyes. Oh, yes, he'd say what he pleased, he'd
weave a bed of thorns. Dola would be a memory of heaven
for Guard Michael Flannigan after *he* was through with him!

Chapter 43

Brendan Donnelly stood on the pavement outside William
Street Barracks and looked through the dark archway
that led to the office marked "Inquiries." It was a cold
day in the end of November, and his collar was raised about
his neck. He had contemplated coming here for several weeks,
on one occasion reaching the door of the office and then
turning around again. He dreaded to cross this bridge, but he
knew that it was all that he had left if he were to find Liam's
killer. He touched the plastic bag in his pocket. It contained
Liam's red neckerchief, so kindly pressed on him by the man
at Priest's Estate. He lowered his collar, took off his hat, and
looked up and down the street. He stepped off the bustling
footpath and into the deserted laneway.

He entered the dayroom where a young Guard sat with a
brown mug in his hand. The man jumped suddenly to his
feet as Brendan entered. "Good day to you," Brendan said.
"It's a shaky day out, isn't it?"

But the young Guard was not to be coaxed by politeness.
Brendan suspected that, where he came from, city niceties
were to be regarded with suspicion. Probably the back of the
beyond. County Clare. Or worse still, Galway. "Would you
state your business?" the Guard said, using the official rote to
cover his accent.

"I'm here to see the Superintendent."

"Do you have an appointment with him?"

"No, I don't."

"Well, it's out of the question then. He's busy. You'll have to state your business to me."

Brendan looked into the red country face. Most certainly County Galway. Not more than twenty-five years of age. He knew the qualifications for the job: muscular body, Primary Certificate, and a letter of recommendation from the parish priest. "Then, if I have to deal with you, lad," he said, "I'll keep my information to myself."

"You will?"

"And tell your man that I'm sorry that I couldn't pass on the word that I have, word on the murder of a boyo. Good day."

"Wait!" the Guard said. "Wait on a bit. I'll see if he's free."

The Guard left the dayroom by the rear door. He was back in seconds. His indifference had changed to a measure of respect. "Your name, sir?" he asked mildly, now.

"Brendan Donnelly."

"He'll be with you in a minute, Mr. Donnelly. He said that you're to wait in his office."

"Thank you."

"Would you like tea?"

"No. Thanks all the same."

As he left the dismal dayroom for the comfort of the Superintendent's office, Brendan remembered a night, years past, when he had sat in the same gray room and could not drink his tea for laughing. He had accompanied Lalla Mack, so that his friend might not be so nervous as he sang "Mona Lisa" over the phone to a mutual friend, Pa Hayes, in Los Angeles, California—one amadan singing to another as a third looked on. Oh, they were simple and innocent days, indeed, he thought as he closed the door behind him.

He had not been seated for more than a minute when the door was opened by Superintendent Meehan. Brendan looked up from his chair. The tall gaunt man above him had an air of severity which was not dispelled when he smiled. "Good day, Mr. Donnelly," he said. "And what might I do for you?"

Brendan watched the gray face. "You remember," he said, "the 'suicide' of Liam Daly, earlier this year?"

"Yes. He was the boy from 'The Field.' The misfortune blew the top of his head off."

Brendan had not expected the compassion. "Well," he said, "he was my friend."

The Superintendent leaned back against the desk. "I know," he said. "I saw you come out of the Daly house the night of the wake."

"You know?"

"You'd be surprised to hear what we know."

"But . . ."

"But why don't we arrest you? That's a good question. The truth is that we have difficulty separating the chaff from the seed. Some of you are just up to pranks, others may set this country on fire from one end to the other before long. To be honest, we're biding our time until we can nab the principals. But, by God, then we'll swoop down like hawks. And don't you forget it."

Brendan shivered. "I didn't come here to be threatened," he said. "I came to ask your help."

"A boyo looking for the Guards' help!" He laughed.

"Yes."

He reached in his pocket and withdrew the red neckerchief from the bag. He placed the cloth on the desk before him. "That," he said, "was Liam Daly's scarf. He wore it the night of his death. It was found caked in blood the following morning."

The Superintendent stood erect. "Where did you get this?" he said.

"From a man who found it near Priest's Estate."

"Priest's Estate. The boy was found on Canal Bank."

"True. It puts a different light on the matter, doesn't it?"

"But are you sure that this was his scarf?"

"I gave it to him last Christmas, I should know. The trademark will bear me out."

"Murder?"

"What else could it be with the body in one place and a bloodied scarf in another? Surely to God he didn't crawl across the mile of fields and marsh to get to Canal Bank. Someone took him there. Whoever it was, killed him."

"But why would they move him?"

"Who knows? The lights, maybe. That area near Priest's Estate is pretty bright. They could have hurt him there—he was on his way out to see me—and then taken him to the darkened bank."

The Superintendent said nothing. He pursed his lips as he turned the scarf over and examined it further. Finally, he said, "Wait on a minute. I'll be back."

When he left, Brendan had the sudden urge to rise up and run pell-mell through the corridor. He'd be in William Street in seconds. From there it would be no time to Laffey's pub . . . Instead, he clutched the arms of the chair, pressing his palms against the wood. He'd stand his ground. He'd stick it out if it killed him.

The Superintendent returned. In his hands he held a brown folder. He sat back on the desk top and leafed through the contents. "We had no way of knowing if he sustained a head injury before the gun was put to his head," he said. "There wasn't much left to examine, God help us."

"You had no doubts at all?"

"None. It was given out that he wasn't the most stable of people. We just naturally assumed that he did away with himself."

"But the scarf is enough for you to open the case?"

"It is—with your help."

The Superintendent scratched the side of his face. "God, though," he said, "I don't know where we're going to go from here." He paused. "You got the man's name who found it, right?"

"Right. Mc Grath from Peter's Cell."

"I suppose we'll have to get a bit of information from him and go back out there to Priest's Estate and have a close look around. But so much time has gone by. Of course, there's the I.R.A. gun. But that had no prints except the boy's . . ."

"Why do you say I.R.A. gun?"

"Because it was such a gun."

"Wasn't it just a Luger that you could pick up at Nestor's . . ."

"Oh, no. No."

"What?"

"Well, that's why we issued our statement declaring that he was I.R.A."

"You're losing me on the gun."

"It was one of a batch stolen in England several years ago. The serial numbers on the bolt and the clip were part of a series—all from the same consignment. We have captured other guns from the grouping."

"But he would have had no gun of his . . ." Brendan stopped.

The Superintendent finished it for him. "Of his own. I see what you're saying—that it was issued to someone for a job."

"I didn't say that."

"You as good as said it. In my day we weren't as organized. We fought with pitchforks and pellet guns—anything that we could get our hands on. No fancy ordnance supplies for us."

"In *your* day?"

"Why, lad," he said, "I was an I.R.A. man when you were nothing more than a glint in your daddy's eye. But we were patriots. We loved this old bit of heather . . ."

"I'm a patriot."

Brendan was out of his chair and reaching for the doorknob when the Superintendent spoke. "Mr. Donnelly," he said, "I know that I can't stop you in what you're going to do. But will you please promise to call us if you find anything?"

His words were lost on the back of Brendan Donnelly as he pushed through the street door and into the alleyway.

Chapter 44

The matter of Guard Michael Flannigan caused Colum some annoyance. He took broad leeway with Riordan's information. Why had Flannigan been transferred to Dola? Was it that there were fewer young girls in the small village? What scandal had been discreetly covered up in Killaloe by parents with influence? What were the immoral liberties taken by this Guard with his young athletes in this city by the Shannon? And now, in his isolation, were his atrocities the frustrations of a man used to more blatantly sexual outlets? However, Colum did not submit the story to meet the first issue in December. There was something left unsaid, he felt, some delicious detail to cap off the concoction. If only he could dredge up one real incident, one prop to set the trick on its head. This would anchor his speculations, turn the village against the fat ox (he vaguely remembered the Guard to be broad and stout—or was that the other one?), and make him the monster of his barracks.

At first he thought of sharing the story with Sean Keane, but at the last minute changed his mind. There'd be others that they could collaborate on. Sean might just not see the point of the thing as he himself did. He might not share his enthusiasm for the gist of it all. It had to be admitted that the boy was new to the paper and also an essayist, not a maker of images in the traditional sense. The latter admission on the part of Sean had bothered him. Still, he seemed to be coming along nicely for all the liabilities. Of course, Colum's own manual had helped.

He went back to his office and pulled the curtains. Where

was the connection, he asked himself. He had spoken to every contact in Killaloe without result. The Guard had been transferred suddenly, nothing more. He put his head on his desk and closed his eyes.

After about a minute, he suddenly raised up. He reached in his desk drawer and found the telephone directory. It was easy to locate the police barracks in the southern sector. Ballina-Killaloe. He had it!

When he had dialed the number, he heard the harsh bell repeat over and over. Were they closed for the day? What day was it? He looked at his calendar—Wednesday, December 1st. Christmas holidays hadn't surely . . .

"Killaloe Garda Barracks," the country voice said. "Guard Yelverton here."

"Garda," Colum almost shouted.

"Yes, sir?"

"My name is Kevin Flannigan. I'm calling from Liverpool. My brother Mick Flannigan is billeted with you there. I wonder if he's in . . ."

"Mike Flannigan?"

"The same."

"Oh, he's not here anymore, sir."

"But I had a letter from him back in June. He was getting along fine. Training the girls' teams . . ."

"He was, then," the Guard's voice dropped.

"Is there anything wrong?"

There was a heavy pause. "Well, I shouldn't be telling you this, sir. But seeing that you're his own flesh and blood . . ."

"Go on."

"It's an official matter—or I should say that it *was*. All hush-hush. But I'll tell you anyway."

"Yes." Colum had difficulty containing his excitement.

"A barrel—it was over a barrel."

"Who had him over a barrel?"

"No. No. A real barrel. Several barrels, as a matter of fact. They found them at the back of Mick's house. They were being delivered by one of the publicans on his route. A bribe. Of course, he didn't get the sack. Instead, they sent him to the back of the beyond, Dola. It was no big thing, really. A lot of others are doing the same. But someone called in on him, and the Super had to make an example. It's the times. A man can't keep nothing to himself."

"It's true."

"Now, I shouldn't have told you all of this, but . . ."

"It'll stay with me."

"Don't say a word to Mike when you talk to him, for Christ's sake. We were very great. You said that your name was Dan, right?"

"Right," Colum lied.

"Weren't you at sea there for a bit?"

"I was."

"You're back, now?"

"I am."

"For good?"

"Yes."

The Guard coughed. "Ah, I'll let you go now. It must be costing you a pretty penny. Good day."

Colum eased the receiver back on the stand and let his breath out slowly. "A fucking barrel of stout!" he said aloud. "The bastard arrested me, and he a drunkard himself."

But what could he make of a few stolen barrels of stout? Nothing. The people of Dola and the surrounding countryside would laugh at the pettiness of *Cumas* if he printed the story. There was only one way—give them what they'd relish. He lifted the original story from its folder and placed it among those that were ready for the print shop.

Chapter 45

As Brendan passed through the dimly lit streets of Adare, he remembered, as he always did, that in this tiny County Limerick town he had kissed the hands of

John F. Kennedy. He could still see him there in his pinstripe suit, the shock of hair blowing in the damp wind, and the people about him as though he were a prince of the realm. Gone were the days. And now they were saying filthy things about him, this last god of the century. Lord have mercy on him, Brendan thought, as he turned into a dark boreen and parked the Morris Minor.

It was a mile, at least, across the fields to "the barn," a dilapidated hayshed that accompanied a similarly run-down farmhouse, halfway on the road between Adare and Kildimo. It was a cover that had never once been liable, simply because the farmer who owned the place, Mick Ginty, gave every outward sign of activity, even allowing the cows and chickens to wander freely through thè covered stalls and bins that stored the munitions for all of West Limerick. That put off, of course, any curious eyes which might have taken interest from a distance. Ginty's personality was the close-up deterrent. It was said that since his wife had died ten years before he had said no more than a handful of words to even the closest neighbor and had made it known that he was not in need of friendship. Why he had ever allowed the organization to use his farm, Brendan could never guess.

As he approached the farmhouse, he saw that only the yard light glowed. The house itself was in darkness. And why not, he thought; it was two o'clock in the morning. The devil himself wasn't up. Brendan had spent most of the day in bed, leaving the house only once to run Josie into Broderick's, the chemist's, for a powder for her stomach. He would be alert for this, he had decided, as alert as he had ever been on an official caper.

He carefully made his way along the southern edge of the farmyard, through the array of broken harrows and rusted ploughs. He knew the ground like a book. He had come here on darker nights than this. Still, he was more nervous now. The fact that he was pitted against some real adversary, capable of taking a man's life, had come home to him. The prankish days of blowing out tires and disrupting traffic were gone. This was what it came down to in the end—one man against another, one man capable of snuffing out another's candle of life. He realized then that his father's pride on those early Easter Sunday mornings was two-pronged—pride at having saved the Republic, and pride at having faced death or danger and come away alive. So it was a bit selfish in the end, he thought, but what wasn't?

Suddenly, he heard the snarl of a dog not twenty yards from him. My Jesus in heaven! He'd forgotten!

He crouched in the darkness. "Blazes," he said. "Blazes. Here, boy. Here."

At first there was nothing. But then he heard the rustle of dry grass. The great black Alsatian came towards him, its tail wagging. The dog licked his face and raised its paw to be petted.

It was easy to find the key to the lower bins. He thought that Bunty Foran might at least change the lock once in a while. The key was the same, a big rusty bolt that might have served to open the vault of a cathedral. They were getting overconfident. The Gardai were being taken for granted. It wouldn't be this way in the North, he thought, remembering the many passwords required to get within a mile of such an armory.

Once inside the underground cage, he switched on his flashlight. He recognized immediately that changes had been made. The bins in the room were piled high with Russian-made rifles and boxes of grenades stamped with other foreign trademarks. He noticed, too, that several cases of dynamite were stacked against the east wall. Were they planning Armageddon? In *Ireland?* He thought of the Superintendent's words. What the Guard wouldn't do with this cache!

When he reached the row of pistol drawers along the north wall, he stopped and examined one of the clipboards that hung on a nail beside each section. The attached invoice indicated, in the left column, the total number of weapons contained in the drawer. The center lines showed those guns issued on particular dates. The right hand section verified the return of these hand pieces. The chart he held was marked "Colts." He moved down the line.

When he reached the Luger closets, he was obliged to stand on his tiptoes in order to unhook the clipboard. When he eventually loosened it, he brought it down into the light. It read like all the others. Total. Withdrawal. Returns. The same as a bloody bankbook, he thought.

He was surprised to find that the invoices indicated a great flurry of activity in the very months when he had thought a lull existed. Buckley had lied to him. They had all lied to him. He leafed through the thick clasp of papers.

Here it was—May. The sheets were already becoming brittle. The first date that caught his eye was May 3, a Monday. Four pistols issued. Four returned the same date. He recalled that caper. The ambush of a Government documents van at Mahoonagh near Newcastle West. The next entry was for May 7, the day of the Mulcahy upset. Three pistols issued. Three returned the same day. That, too, was familiar to him—an early morning shake-up of a Garda station at O'Briensbridge, a diversion for the Annacotty ambush.

He searched for the next entry on a new page but found that at least two weeks were missing from the record. He laid the roster on the ground, unloosened the clasp, and checked each sheet individually. At last he found the misplaced weeks. They had been filed under the entries for the same dates in June.

And there it was, as clear as day—May 8. Two guns issued. But to his disappointment, he also made out the ordnance officer's signature to the right—two guns returned May 9, the next day. He searched his memory. He could not recall any incident related to those dates. Hadn't most of the lads been in William Street Barracks, anyway?

Feverishly, he pulled the heavy drawer from its runners and lowered it onto the earthen floor. He threw back the tarpaulin to reveal the weapons inside. He checked the clipboard. "Total: 35." His fingers grasped the first weapon, and he began to count. "One, two, three, four, five, six . . ."

"Thirty-four," he almost shouted. "Thirty-four." And the empty drawer stared up at him. "I knew it. How could I have been so blind!"

Just then he heard a movement above him. He switched off his flashlight and waited, his heart in his mouth.

There was silence. He could hear the blood pump inside his ribs. The boards creaked slightly as though someone were shifting his weight.

Suddenly, he heard the drunken voice of Mick Ginty fill the emptiness of the barn:

> She's far from the land,
> And she can't swim a stroke . . .

He saw the steaming water come through the boards.

Chapter 46

On a Thursday in early December, when Colum had delivered the stories to the printers, including the one on Guard Michael Flannigan, he returned again to the *Cumas* office. There he found Sean Keane writing a letter. His head was bent forward and he seemed absorbed in his work.

Colum signaled to him. "Come on," he said. "Love can wait. Rosy Mary Cuddahy will pine all the more if you neglect her a bit."

Sean laughed and put his fingers to his mouth. "In a minute," he whispered. "In a minute."

Afterwards, as they drove towards Bennettsbridge, Colum said, "Lord, Sean, but that office is becoming like a second home to you. I'm going to have to watch out . . ."

"Have no fear. It wasn't newspaper business. I quit that at the bell."

"Oh."

They had not drunk in this small town before, and the prospect of finding a new pub at which to celebrate his revenge on the constabulary appealed to Colum. He had thrust out at the stagnant order once again, but this time the effort had been sweeter, more delicious. He thought that he could imagine the mottled face of the Guard as he sipped his morning tea, leafing through the pages of *Cumas* as he did so. Smiling now. The red laughter fading. The frown beginning. A burst of liquid all over the table. The blood rising in the face. A spluttering. But, no. That was too much like a cheap picture. In his mind, he commanded Guard Flannigan to walk into the Dola barracks. The man affected the gruff air of authority (weren't all Guards gruff?). Now he took off his hat and hung it on a nail. "Morning, lads," he said. But the other Guards stayed deep in their mugs and papers. "Has the plague hit?" he said. "Your faces are as long as the night." No. That would not do. It was assigning the oaf the quality of wit and humor. But what if . . . He gave up. It was spoiling his enjoyment. If only a man could control all the components, down to the last exclamation, comma, full stop! If only his words could prove to be more than a distraction, if the victims' actions could be predicted and then observed, with notes made for the future, if words could be made to fashion reality rather than merely color it afterwards . . .

As they sipped their sixth pint and the hands of the clock came together at ten, Colum looked over at Sean Keane. The young man's face seemed pale. He slouched forward in his chair. "Are you all right, Sean?" Colum asked.

Keane sat up. "The drink and the fire made me a little drowsy," he said. "I feel all right, really."

"Too much work. Take a few days off."

Sean was silent. Then he said, "Colum, I've been meaning to talk to you for the last few days. But I haven't gotten around to it. I suppose I should really go to Riordan. But you're close to me, not like a boss at all . . ."

Colum laughed. "More spondulish is it? A raise?"

"No, really."

"How much do you want? You name it. I'll back it to Riordan."

Sean sipped his Guinness. "Thank you, Colum," he said. "It's not that at all. I've got all the money I need. I'm overpaid, actually. *Cumas* should be called *Airgead*, there's so much money floating around."

"What is it then?"

Sean raised his face. "I don't know how to say this," he said. "I know that I've only been here a few weeks. But I'm thinking of leaving—not now, but in a month or two. I've got to. I'll go up to Dublin and find a job on one of the newspapers. In the fall, I'll try my hand at Trinity, get myself a good Protestant education . . ." His voice seemed to hesitate like that of a guilty child caught in some indiscretion.

"Leave? Right when you're catching on in such a grand fashion? A few more weeks and you won't need the manual. You're a born . . ."

"It's no life."

"But you'll be promoted soon. It'll be no time before I am in charge of all of the regions. I can see the handwriting on the wall—Riordan has practically promised me the job of director. I'll bring you with me, right to the top. We'll be a team. The whole country will dance to our . . ." His voice was high-pitched.

"No, thank you, Colum. I can't take it any longer."

"Can't take it? What do you mean?"

"This role we play."

"What role?"

"This pretending to be writers." He put down his glass and leaned forward. "Do you know, Colum," he said, "I sat down last Saturday morning, and try though I might, I couldn't write a decent factual essay on *anything!*"

"Oh, nonsense. It's all in your imagination."

"You've said it!"

"Said what?"

"This. This is imagination. This is an illusory world. But it's Riordan's world, and we are its denizens, his puppets . . ."

"Sean, you've had too much to drink."

"No. Hear me out. We're the pet bonnambhs of the organization. They feed us our prescribed pellets and we shit out our rare and delicate manure. Don't you see?"

Sean was obviously drunk. But Colum chose to answer his argument. "I don't," he said. "All art is a dissembling of reality. The writer and artist draws on the natural world, mixes it with his own creativity, and expels a new and varied reality . . ."

"Colum, propaganda is not art. It never was. It is a semblance of art as a carnival is a semblance of a circus, but lacks the power and pomp and life and grand madness of a circus . . ."

"It depends on the artist."

"Oh, no, it doesn't. Propaganda, in anyone's hands, even yours, Colum Donnelly, is the death of art and the graveyard of the artist. And surely to God, you don't think that those yobs who talk on the phone to us every day are reporting 'the natural world,' do you? A man who accepts another's perception of reality and then builds on it has to be a traitor to art."

"No, you're all mixed up."

"I'm not, Colum. And you're not the first to fall into the whirlpool. I know the fallacy—the mimetic theory gone berserk. Fiction from fiction—the thing that some fools of Yanks claim that they can do by locking themselves up in a college somewhere, their arses warm on scholarships, and by drawing on all the books about them that they've read, not forgetting the witticisms of their other cloistered friends. Their final work is a potpourri of everyone else's experience and not an iota of their own. They are afraid of life—they're like monks. They live in cocoons, white sterile mausoleums of death . . ."

"Oh, fuck you, Sean Keane from Listowel. Who are you? A critic for the *Times*? Art! Art! That's all we ever hear! Every son of a bitch that ever sat at a typewriter talks about *Art*. Do you know what he's really talking about? I'll tell you—power!

And more power! Put a cloak and a crown on him and he'd never write another word. That's what every writer is searching for. But few find it. They linger forever in a limbo. *Half*-gods is all they are, content to suck up to this 'literary' committee and that, this newspaper editor and the next. And what's their reward? A few paltry pounds and the disdain of the mob. *Cumas* gives me the best of both worlds. It offers me the power, and it allows my talent as a writer to go untouched—I have my cake and eat it!"

Sean stood up. "I've had enough for tonight," he said. "My head is swimming. You stay on, Colum. I'll catch the bus on in."

"I'll drive."

"No. Stay on. I feel like the fresh air, anyway."

"Please yourself. You're sure?"

"Sure."

Sean put on his overcoat in silence. When he had buttoned it to the collar, he said, "Do me one favor, Colum."

"Name it."

"Go home and write one of those marvelous stories that you used to submit to the *Irish Times* and *The Press*. I'm sincere when I ask you this. I really and truly want to see if what I've said tonight holds water. Do that for me, will you?"

"No bother. And you, will you do me a favor?"

"Yes."

"Don't say a word about your resignation to Riordan for at least a month."

"A month?"

"Until after Christmas."

"Okay."

Sean lowered his hat over his eyes and stepped into the crisp night air.

Chapter 47

W hen Colum returned from Bennetsbridge, it was well past midnight. He had thought of dropping by Sean's flat, but at the last minute decided against it. The boy had rather annoyed him, to say the least. Here he was, not more than twenty-one, and talking about art as though it were his next-door neighbor. He'd show him, he'd convince him, he'd change his mind about a lot of things. But Sean was immature. The life at *Cumas* perhaps did lack the quality of romance he had enjoyed as the small-town Ben Hecht, trailed after by the likes of Mary Cuddahy and her simple kind. He thought briefly of the adulation that he had felt on receiving the writing award that summer, the adventure of it all. Colum would have to see that some excitement was provided.

He lifted the Adler from the press below his desk. So *Cumas* was a graveyard? Well, if all it would take was one small story to convince Sean, then there was no better time than the present to be about it. His head was clear. The effects of the porter had worn off, cleared by the night's air. Oh, how wrong Sean Keane had been! Certainly, he had not had much time for his own writing, but, nonetheless, he told himself, the ideas were as frequent as ever. Lately, he had been concentrating on the construction of a story in which the time element was completely destroyed, in which the tension arose not out of the traditional mode of narrative links but, instead, out of the immediacy of the values expressed and the "friction of the individual metaphors," as he had heard some American critic explain.

For more than two hours, he constructed the parameters of his story, avoiding with great care the worn-out pitfalls. He had the steps clearly laid out. It was now necessary to drape these bones with cloaks of flesh, and then to watch the entire body shake itself, as it always did, like a boy become accustomed to his First Communion suit. This he did with precision, patting here, plastering there. At last the model was complete, and he stood back and looked at it, widening his eyes, like any artist, allowing the seams to fade and the collection of parts to emerge as an entity. It was done! "See, Sean Keane," he said, "it was easy, easy as pie."

About three o'clock he went to bed, but he could not sleep. He knew that every fiber of the story was intact. But then the doubt arose—would his friend be sophisticated enough to see the innuendoes, the play on words, the leitmotifs, the surface inaction? (After all, he had admitted to being no more than a journalist.) Hadn't he praised the most romantic of the early stories? Would it be the same as bringing the story to someone like Brendan who was still reading *Our Boys* when he was twenty-five and filling up with tears every Christmas when RTE ran *A Christmas Carol?* He wondered, before he finally dropped off to sleep, if, indeed, this was the right story for the occasion, if it would sway Sean in the right direction. Now, he wasn't quite sure.

Chapter 48

Colum was up at seven and back again at the typewriter. The story would not do. He had convinced himself of that. He leafed through his files and came up with a story which he had considered submitting to the National Grants in May. At the last minute, he had luckily made a switch. Why not give *this* story to Sean? What would be the harm in it? He would be doing as his friend had said— writing a story at home. Wasn't he home? Wasn't he here at the typewriter writing? Okay, so it was *copying,* but, by God, it was *writing,* too! He put a clean sheet of paper into the Adler and began to transcribe, changing little of the original.

Later, when he arrived at the office, Sean Keane was

already at his desk. "Morning, Sean," Colum said as he approached.

"Morning," Sean said and turned towards him. "Listen, Colum, I'm sorry about last night . . ."

"I'll hear none of it." Colum put his hand on Keane's neck. "We'll have to do it soon again. I haven't had a good discussion since God knows when. I enjoyed listening to your theories. You got home all right?"

"Oh, yes. Yourself? What time did you leave?"

"Almost right away. I looked for you at the bus stop, but there was no sign, so I drove home." He paused. "Oh, by the way," he said, "here's the story I promised you. I've been up half the night on it, I might add."

Sean Keane looked with astonishment at the brown folder extended to him. "You wrote it last night?" he said. "Jesus, I never meant . . ."

"Finished it this morning."

"Look . . ."

"Don't worry. It was a labor of love. Tell me what you think when you get the chance—and be truthful! I've got to see Riordan."

Sean Keane's face dropped. "Colum," he said, "you're not going to mention . . ."

"Not a word of it. It's between ourselves—two friends."

When he reached his desk, he buzzed Riordan's office. He heard the click, and then the voice answered, "Yes, Colum, what is it?"

"Oh, I was wondering if I might have a word with you? Nothing really important, just a bit of a chat."

"Certainly. See you in the first office."

When Colum reached the cubicle, Taig Riordan was already seated, his feet on the desk. "Sit down. Sit down," the old man said.

Colum sank into one of the soft chairs. "Nothing much," he said. "But I've been mulling over a proposition in the last few days, and I thought that I might talk it over with you."

"By all means—fire away!"

"Well, I've been thinking—and correct me if I'm wrong—that we work here in what might be called an illusory world. And all that is very fine. But what I'm saying is this: wouldn't it enhance our perspectives if, for once, say, we were present at one of the events that we report . . ."

"Yes. I follow. However, the reality might prove dangerous. What if one of you were hurt or captured? Or, what if the real thing proved to be a letdown—the heart of the heart, the holy of holies, as they say?"

"I believe that I would rise above the latter."

"What about Sean—I take it that when you said 'we,' you were talking about him?"

"Yes. It is my concern for Sean that has brought about this subject." He took full study of Riordan's eyes. They seemed to narrow. He continued quickly, "He's young, and I don't think that he has achieved the distance that you and I have so often spoken about. He needs excitement, a sense of derring-do. I can feel it."

"He'll mature in time."

"But the thing is to keep him excited until that maturity comes."

"But what if that tempering proves to be a shambles? I would think that the way to involve him would be through the paper itself. Let him see the power that he has at his fingertips. Show him the responses of the national press to our rhetoric and polish. My God, in the last months you've had compliments coming from even the intellectual critics such as Desmond Heffernan, Phillip Costigan . . ."

"I have, but he hasn't. And it will be some time before I can allow him to handle the important stories and releases. Why did he come to us? To write, to enter into a world of intrigue, and to have a little more money than he'd ever had before. I'm sure you played on this when you brought him in. Right?"

Riordan smiled. "Yes," he said.

"He is different from me. He needs all those three elements. We've given him two. He must have the third."

"You wish to baptize him, put something on his head. It's the priest in you, Colum Donnelly." He laughed. "Go ahead, then. Tell me what you have in mind. You have it all thought out as usual, I'm sure."

"I do."

"I guessed as much."

Colum stretched his legs. "Well," he said, "there's this matter of transporting the man suspected of killing the British ambassador, Ewart-Biggs."

"You mean Dermot O'Murchu?"

"Yes. We have word from two contacts in the Portarlington area that the Guards and soldiers from the barracks in Sallins will transport him to Port Laoise on the Saturday before Christmas. There's a plan to ambush that train, isn't there?"

"There is. But it'll be awfully dangerous. We're using only tried commandos. I wouldn't want yourself or Sean . . ."

"That's not what I'm saying. The way I see it is that we could create a diversion, fabricate a story or a hint, in fact, that would suggest that the rescue might take place at, say, Kildare . . ."

"But they'd know that we were bluffing."

"Not if each regional issue of *Cumas* had a different version."

"You mean to completely baffle them?"

"Why not? What's to lose? They know as sure as the sun is in the sky that an attempt is going to be made and that we're going to make hay out of the event."

"That's right. Confusion would only help our efforts and break their backs, in a way. I could let you in on the official plan . . ."

"I don't want to hear it. It might somehow influence my story. I might subconsciously let something slip, allow the taunt to become too obvious."

"I see. And how will you tie this in with Sean Keane?"

"I'll set up the skeleton of the article. But I'll have Sean write it. In it I'll have him suggest the powerlessness of the Army and Guards to stop us when we have a mind to get things done—the usual. Then I'll have him suggest how we might rescue O'Murchu at Kildare—if we were so inclined. We'll make asses out of them all. Then, to top it off, Sean and myself will drop by to see our handiwork."

"You're a devil, Colum Donnelly. You make it sound so enticing that I almost wish that I could go along myself!"

"Ha!"

Riordan stood up. "You have my full permission," he said. "I'll get to all the other quarters immediately. Good luck to you. This is a big one."

"I know."

Riordan returned to his office and closed the door behind him. Colum sat alone in the cubicle for several minutes before dialing Sean's extension number.

Sean Keane held in his hand the brown folder that Colum had passed to him earlier. "I'm finished," he said. "Every last word."

"Oh," Colum said. "That. It was for something else I called you."

"Jesus, it's great stuff!"

"*That* story?" For a moment he looked away.

"Yes, that story. I'm sorry. It must be my poor talent. This work hasn't hurt you a bit. You're in better form than you ever were. I wish to God that I had your ability . . ."

"Listen, it's not that at all. It's that this place is new to you. You're all cooped up. Another thing is that you haven't had reactions to your work yet; in Tralee you had that all the time. Soon the national press will be talking about *your* stories and opinions as well as mine. The fever will be on you then, believe me. I know! What you need for the time being is a shot in the arm."

"I suppose you're right."

"I know I'm right. And I have the remedy, Sean, the adventure that will set us both on our heels."

"Here?"

"It'll go out from here, and we'll be part of it. The caper of capers. By God, afterwards, we'll take one full weekend in Dublin, and we'll have women and wine and song! But you've got to trust me."

Sean's face had not lost the admiration that had showed on it when he first came in. "I'm with you," he said.

"Then get out there quickly and get yourself a pencil and paper. Do I have something to put on you!"

Sean was up and out of the office in less than a second, it seemed. Colum had already begun to dream the details of their outrageous diversion.

Chapter 49

For as long as he had known Bunty Foran, the ordnance officer had drunk his pint at Humphrey's pub in Lock Quay. You could set your clock by him, the lads often said. Five on the dot he usually left Adare in his battered van, and five thirty he was seated behind the first barrel on the left in the cosy public house. A man of habit. Learned perhaps in his fifteen years as a sergeant in the Irish Army before being courtmartialed and discharged for a trifle. Brendan had heard the story over and over again and knew also the bitterness that went with it.

He entered the premises from a laneway off Old Clare Street. His watch read quarter to six. He felt guilty. It wasn't decent to draw out an old man. But it was the only way. The break-in at Adare had revealed only one thing: the gun found in Liam's hand had been checked out for the purpose of murder and never returned, though the invoice indicated that it had. He had been unable to find the roster of signatures. That was kept in the locked safe behind Bunty Foran's desk, he guessed.

He had no bother recognizing the whiskered little man in the corner. He moved casually past the red barrels and pretended to select a stool at the counter. It was then that he heard the hoarse voice call out, "Brendie!"

He turned. "Oh, Jesus, Bunty," he said. "The dead shall rise again!"

"Come over! Come on over! Bring your pint."

Brendan made a sign to the bartender for two pints and two small whiskies. He hated this. It was mean.

When he had carefully placed the drinks on the barrels, he said, "Well, Bunty, how have you been keeping?"

"Oh, busy, Brendie, busy. Never a minute to myself. And you?"

"Fine. I'm working at the Canal across the street."

"There's good money there."

"And enough of the Black Lady."

"Isn't that right! So tell me, I don't see you out by Adare any more these days. Are you out for keeps?"

Brendan raised his glass of stout and finished the contents. Then, he said, "Maybe. I'm getting a bit old for traipsing around the countryside blowing things up. It's the peaceful life for me now."

Bunty had not touched his whiskey, but now he emptied the glass in one gulp and signaled to the counter for another round.

"No. No," Brendan said. "You'll have me drunk as a lord before I'm finished."

"Drink up. We'll have to celebrate your going away from us. And, to tell you the truth, Brendie, I don't blame you. It's getting awfully hairy this past few months. I'm a little frightened myself. But I'm an old man, what have I to lose? The money is powerful."

"Ah, you have a good responsible job there, Bunty. And you're safe from the danger outside. But I'll bet it's hard to keep track of everything. Jesus, there's no knowing to the cost of all the equipment that passes under your hand."

"You'd be surprised if I told you."

After that, Foran seemed reluctant to speak further of Adare. Some men from Russell's Bakery had entered, and he eyed them cautiously as they sipped their pints and talked loudly at the bar. Brendan did not pursue the subject. He allowed the old man to spout vehemently about the injustices he had suffered at the hands of the Army. However, he made certain that the glasses of whiskey before them were never empty.

At about eight o'clock, the workingmen from the bakery left, and Bunty Foran seemed to relax again. He spoke freely, now, of some of the capers of the past year, mentioning, of course, Brendan's last assignment at Annacotty. "Yes," Foran said, "that was a beaut. You did a professional job, unlike a lot. I remember it well."

"What kind of rifle did I use, Bunty?" Brendan asked.

"Kind? An Armalite, of course. Don't you remember?"

"Just checking the old head. Ha!"

"I remember every job and the guns and explosives used."

"Go on!"

"No. Try me. Ask me anything." The whiskey was in full effect. The time was ripe.

Brendan took it handy. "Let me see," he said, "if I can't rattle your brain."

"Come on! Come on!"

"Okay. What about the caper at Mahoonagh?"

"The one in May? On the documents van? Easy—four Lugers."

"Are you sure?"

"Certain. I have what the Yanks call a photographic memory. I'm so used to them lists that I can see them as if they were fucking streets with houses and children on them."

"Amazing."

"Come on. Try some more on me."

Brendan took another peg from his whiskey and followed that with a large gulp of stout. "I'll tell you what, Bunty," he said, "why don't we go for a pound a guess?"

"Grand. But you'll lose your money like water flowing through those locks of yours over there."

"First question, then. What about the job in Mallow in early April?"

"Easy. Five Smith and Wessons."

"And the raid in Kilmallock just after Easter?"

"Eight Colt 45's."

"Amazing!"

"That'll be two pound, Brendie, me lad."

"Right."

"Once more!"

"That's all I can afford. You're too good, Bunty."

"No, more!"

Brendan's tongue wet his lips. "I've got it," he said nervously. "I heard from a reliable source that the night after the Guards arrested the lads from the parish, a job was pulled right there and then."

Foran seemed to draw up. He squinted his eyes. "Well, Brendie," he said, "you heard a rare one. It's not much that the big lads let out about themselves, and I never ask, just do me duty."

Brendan retreated. "I won't ask you that one, then," he said quickly. "Let me guess at another caper . . ."

"No. Hold on. For Christ's sake, you're one of my own. And as you said, you know the details anyway, though I wouldn't be going around telling them to anyone. Do you hear that?"

"I do."

"Two Lugers. Taken out just before I left 'the barn' that Saturday night. And put back and signed in and everything when I came to work on Monday morning."

"But I thought you checked in everything yourself?"

"When it's one of the boyos that brings something back, they have to leave it there on the desk for me to check it."

"One of the boyos?"

"Yes. Like yourself."

"But who's *not* a boyo? I don't follow . . ."

"Sure, Jesus, Brendan, are you stupid or something?"

"What do you mean?"

"The Boss . . ."

"McDavitt?"

"Himself."

"Alone?"

"The pair of them. Himself and the top lad."

He took several seconds to ask the question. "Riordan?" he said finally.

"The very face of death himself."

He felt empty inside, as though the very life had been taken out of him. However, he tried desperately to talk of other things, his job, the weather, the drop in the pound. He could not afford to leave an ounce of suspicion in Bunty's drunken brain. None whatsoever.

In his room, later, he tried to sort out the muddle of it all. Who was Riordan? Not an Irishman. Now that might be the clue again. But he stopped. What was he? A maker of excuses? A signer of notes that said this and that and he and she were without blame? It was as plain as the light of day—McDavitt, O'Murchu, and the others—all as native to him as the ground beneath his feet, and one man as deadly as the other, and as compassionless. He saw the true meaning of their brotherhood. These hoodlums were linked and welded together as gears and cogs and braces are welded in an engine of destruction. They cared little for each other but loved desperately what each man held high—chaos, upheaval, the letting of blood in the false name of some vague patriotism from the forgotten past, some lost banner, some untranslatable catch phrase emblazoned in harps and shields and scepters. Where had they come from? Certainly they were not the descendants of men such as Pearse and Clark and the other long-dead heroes of 1916? No. They had come out of the forties and fifties, out of the drudgery and housing scheme warrens of those days. Only in the beginning there was religion with all of its "shalt nots" and nagging guilts and containments which halted a man before he crossed the thin line that separates him from the mongrel on the street, ready to give fight for the sake of a filthy bone or because of the pain and inclemency of the day. Ah, but now, those ancient terrors were gone. The churches were empty. The confraternities disbanded. The pilgrimages full of the old and deformed. The organization was no longer content to play its stirring music on street corners or to whisk the children of the poor off of a Sunday to Coolea or Galway for a day's harmless outing of singsong and games. This was now the reign of Give-Me, and the movement was its god, and the movement knew its followers like the palm of its hand. The day of the man of heart was in its twilight. These faces that he was familiar with could no longer be rightly called Irish or Catholic, they belonged to no particular nationality or faith. They were a breed, a breed that had to be castrated if its line were to be stopped. And he knew that it would only come with holocaust as it had always come before when the abscess broke above the flesh of history and called itself Nero or Cromwell or Hitler or whatever tag it chose. The man in the street would do nothing about it until it poisoned his tea and routed him from his house. To him, the Provos and their like were a mere puzzle: on one hand he called them terrorists, and on the other he reluctantly gave lip service to their daring and insolence. Because, inside of himself was a strain of the same seed as theirs. And Brendan Donnelly knew that he would never be able to dissever himself completely from its deceit or confound the cancer that was already in the blood. But from this day he would try.

Chapter 50

Several days before the lark at Kildare, Colum received a letter from home. However, when the postman handed it to him, he was already late for an appointment with Riordan. They planned to put the final touches on the vital *Cumas* article of that week. Before closing the door, he placed the envelope behind the holy water font that the previous tenant had erected. He'd attend to it when he came home.

It was two days before he thought of it again. When he did, he tore the envelope open with his ungloved hand and began to read the first page. Josie had nothing much to report. Her stomach was giving her a bit of trouble—she'd have to have Dr. Holmes (did Colum know that the man's instruments had been blessed by the Pope?) look at her after Christmas. And speaking of the holidays, when would he be home? His room was all prepared for him—Brendan had helped herself and their mother put up a bit of bright wallpaper and lay a nice piece of carpet on the floor. Would he be able to make it by that Friday, Christmas Eve? It would be lovely for all of them to go to Midnight Mass at St. Mary's and then rush home in the snow (it was already working itself up to a grand fall) for a feed of rashers and bacon and pudding. But even if he made it by Christmas morning, they'd at least be together for the family dinner—ham, turkey, plum pudding, oyster soup . . .

He folded the letter. Josie and her food! He felt his stomach wrench. When had he had a sandwich last? Yesterday? He couldn't recall. He'd cook himself an egg. That'd fill him. An egg and a few cups of Irel coffee.

When he finished his small meal, he decided to answer his sister's letter. Otherwise, it might not get to Limerick in time for Christmas, what with the rush and delay. If that happened, all the fat would be in the fire. "Family"—the all-numbing word—would be thrown up to him the rest of his life.

He began to type. In his letter, he said that he had looked forward to the few days at home, but unfortunately his superior at the *Kilkenny Herald* had put him on call that Friday, Saturday, and Sunday of the Christmas weekend. There was no way at all that he could change it. He was new on the job, and all juniors had to take their punishment.

However, he might have a chance to drop by at New Year's, though he doubted that, too. He was enclosing their gifts and hoped that they enjoyed themselves on him. He included Brendan in his generosity as though one might give a fiver to a man on the street and think nothing of it, knowing that it was only one note from a bundle, and realizing, too, had he been so disposed, that some spiritual reward might be gained by the altruism. In his own case, it avoided conflict. And, to be honest, he had thought little of his brother in recent weeks. He had forgotten the altercation simply because he had surpassed the limits of its influence. He was miles ahead of poor childish Brendan, light years into the future and all that even the most glorious dream could hold for the other. Had he wanted to—God forbid!—he could at any time call for the other's death or dissolution. The thought allowed him such superiority and indifference that he even included another ten pounds for Brendan.

He sealed the letter and sat back. He looked at the bare flat around him. It was a cell, really, an extension of the greater cell of *Cumas*. Lord, in a way, he was like one of those ancient and powerful hermits of his race. St. Kevin. St. Columbanus. And who was that one that had lived on those islands in the Shannon—Scattery Islands? The one that banned women from his domain and put a curse on the head of any one of them that stepped onto his fist of rock and storm! Oh, Jesus, they were grand mad mad fuckers!

He began to visualize Christmas in this place and at the office. (He really had not lied to his sister. After the triumph on Saturday, his days and nights would be filled with work. Riordan would expect this of him. The old man had already coded the assignment. "The Gift of the Magi," he'd called it.) It would be like no Christmas he had ever known. It would be his first away from home. He thought of the imposed separation and saw himself as part of the portraits of desperate Christmases he'd seen on the screen. He remembered, too, that the Master of Novices at Melleray had told him that the first Christmas in the cloister was the hardest one. It was

one of the great trimmings that separated the young pos-
tulant from the world. Many failed to survive the hardship.

He put on his coat. He'd catch the early post.

Chapter 51

W hen Brendan arrived home on Thursday night, he
found Josie crying by the fire. Their mother stood
above her. They both looked in his direction as he
unlatched the half-door.

"What's going on here?" he asked sternly.

Josie did not answer but continued to sob. The mother
spoke. "Children," she said to no one in particular. "You
raise them up and then what do they do? Turn on you and on
each other."

"Speak to the point, woman," he said. "Say what it is."

"It's Colum," she answered quickly. "She just got a letter
from him."

"Is he hurt? Sick?"

"Oh, no. Not that. It's him that's doing the hurting by not
coming home for Christmas."

"Not coming home?"

"No. His hoity-toity job won't let him, he says."

"What's he talking about? Sure there's no job that works
over the holiday—not even Guinness's or Ranks, and they're
Protestants and Jews. If they show respect, who is it that
doesn't?"

"The *Kilkenny Herald*, it seems."

"Oh, is that so?"

He went across to Josie and put his arm about her neck.
"Don't fret," he said. "I'll have a talk with him. With all his
money he can surely pay someone who is hard up to cover
for him."

"But how will you get ahold of him, Brendie?"

"By phone, of course. What are phones for?"

"But you've never used a phone to call far away and . . ."

"So I put two pence in and ask for the operator. Or go on up to Cruise's and have the girl do it for me. My God, do you think that I live in olden times?"

"When will you call him?"

"Tomorrow on my lunch. Jaggers and myself have to stop off at Joe Malone's pub in Denmark Street. I'll run on up and call from Cruise's then."

"Be sure to tell him that we're all expecting him, that we're having his favorite kind of ham, and . . ."

"I'll tell him, the . . ."

When he locked his room door behind him, he took a brown paper bag from his pocket. He opened it. The heavy red box inside tore through the paper and fell to the floor, spilling its 7.65-mm. shells all over the lino. Carefully, he retrieved each one, first filling the Luger clip and then putting the remaining shells back into the carton. He slid the clip into the pistol. It locked with a sure click. In all his capers, he had never used a Luger. There was something about its being German, some touch of failure and condemnation that he could not explain. He wondered as he looked at its bright shiny metal if Bunty would ever miss it or its partner in William Street Barracks. And if he did, would he be likely to make the shortage known? He wondered, too, when the right time would come to use it? Soon? He'd bide his time until everything was perfect, until the two blackguards were firmly in his grip.

As he sat in the dark telephone kiosk in the lobby of Cruise's Hotel, he watched the guests drift in and out. Ruddy-faced farmers. Old women with gaudy hats. Pig and cattle buyers. Pool players dropping in to use the marble jakes. All acting the posh. Walking arrogantly across the frayed and soiled carpet as though this were their castle and the iron railings without were a sort of moat that excluded the uninitiated. Lord Jesus! even the porters were infected with the disease, strutting like bantam cocks in the corridors and vestibule. Wasn't life funny, in a way? What was it the fellow said? "There's only two places where we're equal—when we're in sorrow and when we're on the chamber pot." Ah, but people were people, he conceded. They had their days. There was no point in being bitter.

The girl behind the counter beckoned to him to raise the receiver. He felt his heart jump in his chest. He put the black object to his ear. He heard the voice at the other end say, *"Kilkenny Herald. Kilkenny Herald."* (It sounded like the call of a paper boy on some windy corner.)

"Kilkenny Herald?"

"Yes. Yes. Can I help you?"

"Right. I'm looking to speak to Mr. Colum Donnelly. He's with your paper. Went to work for you this summer. Fall, I mean."

"Donnelly?"

"He's from Limerick. Donnelly. Colum."

"Are you sure it isn't O'Donnell? We have a Brian O'Donnell."

"No. Donnelly. He was a prizewinner last summer in the . . ."

"Let me look at the list. He must be new. I don't have any recollection of a Donnelly."

The line seemed dead for a few minutes, and Brendan was just about to hang up and have the girl at the counter ring again. Then the voice came clearly over the line. "Donnelly, you said?"

"Colum Donnelly."

"We have nobody by that name here."

"You're certain?"

"I'm sure. This list was just made up last week."

"There's no other paper with a name like . . ."

"None. We're it."

Brendan breathed heavily. Realizing the futility of what he was about to say, he said it anyway. "He told us that he had to work over the Christmas. Friday, Saturday, and Sunday."

"Sure, man, we're not even open those days. This place is a graveyard from Christmas Eve to the day after St. Stephen's. Not even the cleaning woman shows her face."

"Thank you very much."

"Quite all right. You simply must have gotten the wrong . . ."

What in heaven was going on? The postmark on the letter said Kilkenny. Colum's talk of the town had been accurate (Brendan had spent several weeks there when he was in the L.D.F.). He was mystified. But he decided to keep the matter to himself until he got to the root of it. There was little use in causing an uproar.

Chapter 52

Colum had slept little during the night, and now as the dawn broke, he sat in his kitchen sipping a lukewarm cup of American coffee. He considered again the details of the plan. The three other editions of *Cumas* had indicated different locations. The northern paper had pointed to Droicead Nua, the western to Portarlington, and the eastern to Monasterevin. He had stuck to his original choice—Kildare. He and Sean would drive to that midlands town later in the morning and then the grand finale would begin. He could already imagine the wide expression of amazement on his friend's face, the utter disbelief that it could all be possible from a few mere paragraphs . . .

He looked at the week's edition of *Cumas* on his lap. The copies had been distributed on street corners throughout Munster the evening before. A mere twelve hours ago. In that time alone, the stirring had begun. He could sense the movements of the thing, slow but certain. What was the word that Yeats had used?—"slouching." Word had come to him of Garda alerts as far away as Ennis, County Clare. The Army, too, had increased its forces along the railroad line. He wondered where Riordan would make his move. Droicead Nua? Monasterevin? Portarlington? Port Laoise itself? Oh, the glory of it!

He concentrated on his part in the great deception. He felt now as he had so many times in the past—before entering an event in a regatta, or taking an important examination, or going to Confession, or standing before his classmates to interpret a difficult passage from Shakespeare or Chaucer. And, as then, his stomach tightened like a vise. The sour coffee surged into his throat. He clutched his mouth in desperation and rushed into the toilet. He spewed the brown-red liquid into the commode.

On the drive north, they were both quiet except in Abbeyleix when Sean pointed out a police van that had stopped by the curb, its blue light flashing. Several uniformed Gardai sat inside eating sandwiches and drinking from white paper cups. "It's a great deal protecting they'll be doing today," Sean said and laughed.

"Isn't it true!"

"Aru from Cork? I am, aru? How's the potatoes? Big and small. How do you ate them? Skin and all."

Sean's imitation of the typical Guard's accent made Colum laugh so much that he had to wipe his eyes with his handkerchief. "Ignoramuses," he said finally.

When they reached Kildare and Colum began to maneuver the Volkswagen through the heavy traffic, he realized that he had made a miscalculation—he had forgotten that Saturday was Market Day. He cursed as he stopped for donkeys and carts, wheelbarrows, tinkers of every cut and figure, and cattle that made the road their own, ignoring the

sprites of men who shouted and cajoled and cursed them
from behind, swinging great crooks this way and that, almost
braining the heads of passersby.

Sean seemed to enjoy the melee, which irritated Colum. "I
didn't come here to look up the arses of sheep and cattle," he
muttered.

"Ah, they all bring back memories of Mary Cuddahy.
Ripe. Large . . ."

"Fuck you, Sean Keane."

At last, on their second drive through the marketplace,
Colum found a tiny space and parked the Volkswagen. His
map indicated that they were only minutes from the train
station.

Before stepping into the railroad square, Colum stopped in
the middle of the cobblestoned laneway. He reached in his
pocket and took out a large pair of horn-rimmed glasses.

"Where did you get those?" Sean asked.

"Woolworth's."

"Oh, Jesus Christ, Colum, what are we? Two master
spies?"

"There's no harm in being careful."

"Do you have a black moustache, too?"

As they approached the middle of the square, Colum felt a
drop of rain fall on his face. He looked up into the gray sky.
As he did, he noticed a movement near the chimney of one
of the shops. On closer examination, he realized that every
rooftop had its tiny figures pressed close against the bal-
ustrades and chimneys and buttresses. Sean, too, had
noticed. "Jesus!" he whispered, "the place is swarming. Don't
look right away, but the laneways are blocked with Garda
vans. They must be expecting an all-out attack."

"And there's only us! Ha!"

This was it! This was what all the posturing and arranging
and blending had come to. And to think that only a few
months before he had actually been awed by Brendan's
cheap mean little ambush at Annacotty. Shit! This was the

pinnacle, the height of the mount. And it was only one of the stations! His brain wave had gotten this soldiery out of their beds, away from the sweet backsides of their wives and lovers, out of the glawm of their children, far from the arms of their fathers and mothers. They were his puppets, they and their commanders. He was their master, standing here on this stage of cobblestones. He had them in his fist. He felt like shouting, shouting in the cant of a childish game, "You're down! You're down! Come out! Come out!"

They approached the granite steps of the station. The ramp above them was deserted except for a wrinkled little man who stood next to an ice-cream cart. Colum cleared the steps in one jump. He reached in his pocket as he came up to the vendor. "Two big fucking cornets," he said. "And ladle on the ice cream."

The man looked puzzled, but he obeyed, piling on the pink cream until it dripped down over the waffled biscuit. He handed the first cone to Sean and the second to Colum. "Two and six," he said.

Colum offered him a fifty pence piece. "Keep the change," he said.

"Thanks, mister. The best of luck to you."

Inside the station, an empty bullet-nosed train stood hissing on the tracks. Great clouds of steam wafted across the deserted platforms. A tobacconist opened the shutters of his kiosk and began to untie the bundles of newspapers on the counter. In a far corner, an old man carefully raised and lowered the lever of a tin imprinting machine.

Sean's face was strained. "This place gives me the creeps," he said. "I have a feeling that we're being watched. It's frightening."

"I told you! I told you it would be exciting . . ."

"We've had our laugh, Colum. Let's get out of here. The least thing might bring the roof down on us."

"No. No. We must relish this, devour . . ."

Suddenly, a voice boomed over the station loudspeaker.

"Attention! Attention!" it said. "Cease alert. Cease alert."

"Damn Riordan," Colum cried. "It isn't time yet! It isn't time yet! Just five more minutes!"

"It's over," Sean said. "They've done the job somewhere else. Let's get out of here before we're picked up for questioning."

From outside, they heard the sounds of lorries and vans as they rumbled across the square. The latest upset was over. They were returning to the safety of their compounds and barracks.

"Jesus, Colum, let's go!"

"No. No. I won't be cheated!" And he dashed away from the grip of his friend, running zigzag up and down the platform, the cornet in his fist and raised above his head. He opened his eyes wide and absorbed the gaudy images of the station—golden beaches of Nice, roasted skins of Clover Meat sausages, big-breasted German girls in lederhosen, aqua fluoride toothpaste oozing from its leaden tube, tangy Canadian bacon sizzling in black frying pans . . .

Without warning, he began thrusting the half-empty cornet at Sean, spilling the milky ice cream. His friend wiped some of the drops from the front of his coat. "Colum," he said, "are you drunk or what?"

"Drink. Drank. Druken. Dring. Drang. Droo." As he spoke, he leveled the biscuit at each billboard in turn.

He was about to make his jongleur's sweep again when a harsh voice spoke above his own. "Halt, there!" it said. "Halt!"

They both turned in time to see two uniformed Guards walk towards them from the direction of the jakes. "O Merciful Jesus!" Sean said.

Colum saw clearly the wild and irritated eyes of the Guards as they approached. The one man small. The other big and stout. He felt the terror rise in his throat and throttle him.

Sean was saying, "Let's stand still. They have nothing on us. Stand . . ."

In that instant, he noticed the light of a stile to his right. In a sudden burst, he dashed towards it. He heard the frenzied call behind him, "Halt! I said halt!"

He was in the stile, madly twisting with its creaky bars. He looked back over his shoulder to see the low-sized Guard drop to his knees. But now the terrified face of Sean blocked the man from view. His friend's hand was out as though he meant to grasp the bars of the turnstile and pull himself through the heavy air towards safety. Just then he heard a dull pop like the release of a pellet gun. Sean cried out and fell across the bars. He saw the blood spurt from his friend's mouth as the boy's face went down through the tangle of steel.

He had no feeling in his legs. He knew only that they were moving him closer and closer to the maze of laneways off the station square. He didn't look back. His life depended on his reaching the confusion and barter of the marketplace. He must not be caught, he told himself. He must not be caught.

Chapter 53

When Brendan returned home on the evening of the telephone call to Kilkenny, Josie met him in the gap. "Did you get ahold of him?" she asked. "Will he be home now?"

He looked into her pale face. He remembered that she had missed two days' work in the last week. Nothing would do her but to go back time and time again to the chemist's for one powder after another, never hearing a word about going to a doctor's office or stopping off at Barrington's. "No," he said, "he was out. I'm to call back tomorrow."

"But wouldn't he be back today?"

"No. He was out on a story."

"But you left a message for him to call . . ."

"Josie, I called him. He wasn't there. I didn't leave a message. Where would I have him call, I ask of you? I'll call him tomorrow. I promise you."

He put his arm about her shoulder. "You'll catch your death going about like this," he said. "Not a coat or a rag on you."

"Sure I *won't!*"

"You will. Especially the way you've been feeling . . ."

"Don't talk about it. I'm all right." She broke away from him and ran through the open door.

Chapter 54

How many hours had passed since he'd left the square and sought the safety of the marketplace? He didn't know for certain. He was only aware of the terror and the cold as he had moved through the throngs of people, pretending to look at the wares of hawkers, touching this and that in the semblance of curiosity, always keeping his eye on the lanes that led in the direction of the station, dreading that the crowds would disperse and leave him paralyzed and alone. But that had not happened. Neither had the Guards appeared.

Now, he finally felt secure enough to search out the Volkswagen. He left the milling afternoon shoppers and found the cul-de-sac where he had parked the car. Somehow, in his imagination, he had expected it to be surrounded by police. But there it stood, safe, untouched, the same as he had left it.

Once inside the safety of the locked doors, he started the engine and leaned back. He reached for the radio knob and dialed the RTE station. The music of Bach flooded the car. He was exhausted. He felt like sleeping.

He must have dozed for a few minutes. When he came out of his stupor he heard the voice of the news announcer:

> For all of their preparations, the Gardai and
> Army were unable today to prevent the rescue by I.R.A.
> Provisionals of Dermot O'Murchu, the terrorist
> suspected of killing the former British ambassador, Mr.
> Ewart-Biggs. The rescue took place at a country
> crossing outside of Sallins. I.R.A. sources had boasted
> earlier that the incident would occur at one of
> the stations along the railway line between Sallins and
> Portlaoise . . .
>
> Gardai shot and killed a man today in the town
> of Kildare. The victim and his companion had been
> called upon to halt and refused. Gardai fired,
> killing one man. The other escaped. Police speculate that
> the men had intended to deface . . .

He turned the radio off. He was safe and his friend, Sean Keane, was dead somewhere. O Merciful God in heaven, what was he going to do?

Chapter 55

On Saturday night after he had finished his supper, Brendan sat back in his chair. He was still pondering the mystery of his brother's whereabouts. He had had to lie to Josie again today, saying that Colum had gone home by the time he'd gotten off at the Barrel Yard and on up to Cruise's to make the call. There was only one thing for it, he decided. He'd have to drive down to Kilkenny one night this week. He'd be back by morning.

He opened the *Independent.* The pages were full of Dermot

O'Murchu's rescue. My God, what cunning, he thought, as he read of the diverse taunts in the week's editions of *Cumas*. The movement had made proper amadans of the civil authorities. You had to hand it to the organization, sometimes. They had the brains at the top. However, he did not allow this praise to change his mind on Riordan and McDavitt. No. Those blackguards would pay, very soon. He was only waiting for the perfect opportunity, the foolproof plan.

Several copies of *Cumas* lay untouched in the wicker basket by the fire. He wondered why they delivered the editions to his house when he was no longer considered an active member. A reminder of his isolation from them? Perhaps. You couldn't be up to them.

He reached for the recent copy and turned to the editorial page. It was all there. A complete concoction. A prediction of a caper that never came to pass. Kildare. And in a moment of weakness, he wished that he could hand the paper to his brother, and say, "Now there's a story for you—a real fiction."

His eyes fell on the line at the top of the new page. The words seemed to stand out from the rest. He read aloud:

> . . . as impotent as yellow china dogs
> above the mantel, as empty as they,
> as foolish as their blue blind stares,
> as useless as the times they stand for.

Slowly, he raised his face. The two brittle ornaments which had been in the family since his father's childhood stood on the ledge above him. China dogs. To be had nowhere anymore. Like pure gold. Their eyes brought back for him the memory of Riordan's face. He saw the gash of mouth say, "Your precision and his voice." *Voice.* Could it be? It was one in a thousand chances. One in a million.

Chapter 56

Colum went directly to *Cumas*. Everything was as he had left it the evening before. Rough drafts of the editorial on the desk. The maps of the midlands town. Even the weather forecast from the previous afternoon. Lord, Jesus, he thought, if only it were possible to obliterate it all, to throw the papers with all their words in the wastebasket and say that it never happened. To walk across to Sean's desk and whisper, "Let's have a pint. Too much work is bad for us. I've decided to forget about the caper. Too risky." But the setting of such a stage was resisted by the empty lighted space at Sean's desk. And he found to his consternation that he was incapable of summoning from the past even the vaguest image of his friend by which to soothe the impotency that he now felt.

Just then, he noticed a brown envelope perched against his telephone. He picked it up and opened it. The glossy contents caught the light. Two large Polaroid photographs. Both of Dermot O'Murchu. Sneering up at him. Free. Alive. Taken here at the office. (He recognized the backdrop.) He felt the blood rush to his face. Why had Riordan done this? Why had he allowed this scum to defile this center, this place . . .

A note fell from behind one of the photographs. He lifted it from the floor. It read:

> Great work! Must lie low for several days. Try
> to get on the story immediately. Go all out on our
> intelligence, superiority, mastery . . . Make utter
> laughingstocks of them. But need I tell you? You are far
> from being an apprentice.

Colum read no farther. What did this mean? Could it be possible that Riordan hadn't heard of Sean's death, of his own fatal blunder in running? He knew of every stir, every move in the country. Why not this? Something was strange.

He walked to the far end of the room. He looked up at the black plastic radio on its bracket above the tea tray. The dial was set on the RTE station. Slowly, he leaned against the wall and put his hand on top of the small box. It was warm.

So this was the heart of the matter—the manipulator being manipulated like a simple detail of a report from the outside. What was Riordan trying to impress upon him, what reasons lay behind the curious pretense? Was it to remind him that the life of the whole was greater than the sum of the parts? Or was it to lure him away from the natural temptation of sorrow and back to the absorbing dazzle of his own importance? Still more seriously, was it to say without saying that he was now baptized and brother, at last, to all the passionless men and gray ghosts who moved like marionettes to the organization's command? And in the end, was this erasure of reality, this deliberate omission, a form of official absolution of error, like saying, "Don't fret. We'll forget about it."

He tore the letter to shreds. He looked about the silent emptiness of *Cumas*, at the gray walls, the yellow lighted desks, the dark cubicles at the rear. What was it Sean had once said? *Mausoleum.* The image bore in upon him, and he thought that suddenly the very air was being drawn out of this buried cavern, that he was being suffocated and divested of his life, that some ominous plot was in motion to murder him. He rushed for the door. The knob seemed to slip beneath his fingers. The sweat stood out on his forehead. But at last the lock clicked. He was up the dark stairs. He was out into the cold air. Breathing. Breathing great gulps of air. The door slammed behind him. And the lights in the vault below burned on.

Chapter 57

Mಉore than an hour later, Colum stood on the landing
of a tenement house in the northern quarter of
Kilkenny. On either side of him, he heard the
raucous laughter of children. Occasionally, the voice of an
adult intruded, uttering some blasphemy, but the laughter
continued, undaunted. Was this the right address? He looked
in his wallet. The slip of paper said: 8 Belvedere Terrace.
This was it.

He climbed the last three steps. Sheila's door faced him on
the next landing. He paused for a minute, then knocked.

He was about to turn away when the door opened slightly.
He saw nothing but heard a girl's voice say, "Who is it?"

"Colum Donnelly. Does Sheila . . ."

The door closed in his face. He heard the rattle of a chain.
It opened again. Sheila was framed in the space, her hair
about her shoulders, a dressing gown held together at her
waist. "Colum," she said in a whisper. "My God, it's been
months—how many?"

"Four."

"It must be more."

"Just four."

"What are you doing here? In Kilkenny. I mean . . ."

"I've been here."

"I knew it! I knew it!" she said. "I thought I saw you leave
Raleigh's in Bennetsbridge one night a few weeks ago. But
when I got outside you were gone. I thought that my eyes were
playing tricks on me."

"They weren't. I was there with my friend."

"See, I was right!" She pulled the gown close about her.
"And now, Colum Donnelly," she said, "tell me why you
waited this long to come and see me?"

"It's a long story. But I'll tell it better if you let me in out of
the cold."

A change came across her face as though she had allowed herself some sunlit reverie and was now suddenly withdrawn from its comfort. "Colum," she stammered. "There's a bit of a problem, really. Could you come back in about an hour? I'll have finished my bath then. I'll be ready. The house won't be in such a . . ."

Right then, a man's voice spoke a distance behind her. "Sheila," he said, "what's going on out there? Tell them we don't want any."

She smiled weakly and bit her lip. "I'm sorry," she said. And she reached out and touched the sleeve of his coat.

"It's all right, really."

"Be good to yourself."

"You too."

He closed the door of his car and started the engine. In minutes he was out of the city. He estimated that with the night drive he would be in Limerick before eleven.

Chapter 58

When Colum drove into the gap, he noticed that the house was in darkness. He parked the car near the shed, and walked to the back door. It was locked. He no longer carried a key.

At first, he thought of knocking but decided against that. He'd only wake the whole house. Instead, he walked around to the front. He began tapping lightly on Josie's window. "Josie," he whispered, "it's me, Colum. Open up."

But there was no answer, only the sharp sound of his sixpence as it struck the hard glass.

Suddenly, he heard the rustle of bushes behind him. He swung around to face into the blinding glare of a flashlight. He felt the old terror take grip of him. "Who is it?" he asked.

At first there was no response, and he knew again the paroxysm he had experienced at the train station when he looked back upon the stout Guard with the bulging red eyes. The silhouette behind the light seemed to increase. The images in his brain came together at last in words. He knew now the source of his recreancy when he cried out, "Guard Flannigan? Guard Flannigan?"

"Just me," a girl's voice said. "Just me, Colum. Ellen Sullivan."

"Oh, God, you frightened me."

"Did you think I was a Guard?" she said and laughed.

"Well . . ."

"I've been waiting in my car for about an hour. I knew you'd come."

"What are you talking about? I just happened to drive up . . ."

"Didn't the Red Cross get ahold of you?"

"No. Why, what's the matter?"

"Josie."

"Josie? What in God's name . . ."

"She's in Barrington's. She collapsed uptown tonight. They rushed her to the hospital immediately. I'm afraid it's serious. They had the priest in."

"Jesus!"

"I told your mother I'd wait for you. They're all inside at the ward."

"Let's go."

"Right."

They climbed the steps of Barrington's Hospital and stood for a moment under the blue light as they waited for the night porter to answer the bell. A cold wind buffeted them. Colum could hear the tide on the Abbey make its run for the sea. He looked at Ellen. She was muffled in a fur-collared coat. She almost looked French in the little tam that sat cocked on the side of her shiny brown head of curls. He touched her shoulder with his gloved hand as the door was opened by an unshaven old man.

The night matron at the desk directed them to a waiting room off the main corridor, and, as they walked towards it, Colum noticed the full chamber pots on every side, the medicine trays strewn carelessly with bottles and needles and soiled towels. And he remembered what Sean had said of Irish hospitals once—that you'd have to be in perfect health going into one so as to come out half alive. Poor Sean. The feeling inside him changed little when he thought of his sister. Poor Josie. He hoped that she'd be all right. He dreaded the details as he pushed open the door of the waiting room.

Inside the room, the faces of the family were instantly paralyzed as he entered. In that second before they spoke and came alive to him, he saw his mother, seated by the window, her eyes like great dobbers in her head, a handkerchief in her fist. But she was not crying. To her right sat Seoirse Hayes. He was a pathetic sight as he shook with convulsive sobs, drinking his tears and wiping his eyes with a patterned rag. Above the fat man, he saw the massive frame of Brendan, slouched against the lighted wall, his face stern.

The mother was the first to speak. "So you got here," she said. "It took a tragedy to bring you home. What if I was going to my grave, or your brother Brendan? Bad 'cess to you and your fancy words and letters and job . . ."

"Stop it, woman. Stop it!" It was Brendan who spoke. "Leave him alone. He's here. That's better than not being here. He came when he could."

"How is she? What's gone on?" Colum asked.

The mother spoke again. "Didn't the Red Cross tell you when they got ahold of you? Or didn't the man at the newspaper pass on the information to you when Brendan called? They said that you'd be back in the office within an hour, there at the *Herald* or whatever it is you call it . . ."

He looked at Brendan. So his brother knew and had chosen to keep silent. He saw the slightest movement of the other's head. Say nothing. "No one got ahold of me, Mama," he said. "I drove up just to come home."

Brendan answered his original question. "Ellen probably sketched what happened for you," he said. "She fell as she was going down the steps of Todd's. Her appendix had been giving her a lot of bother. It burst, we think. They have her down in the operating theatre now. We should hear any minute. It's been a few hours."

"But why this pigsty? Why not St. John's?"

"She was shifted on the spot. Those that picked her up saw that she was an ordinary misfortune. You have to look prosperous to get into St. John's, you know. You might get in yourself, Colum, but the rest of us barely qualify for this place. And it's as good a place as any. Dr. Raya assured me that she would have the best of care."

"An Indian?"

"What's wrong with that? My skin is no whiter than his." He held up his hands which were stained in dirt and the dark red dye of the barrels.

Colum knew that he had little authority here anymore. It was like crossing an international border and foolishly trying to convince the guards that in the country from which you came you were revered and commanded great forces. He had often pondered that notion in Catechism. How Christ had stood before Pilate, and had spoken of a kingdom incomprehensible to the Roman legate. And not gifted with the wisdom of the centuries and the suffusion of the heart, the governor of Judea must have smiled to himself and said, "Poor miserable soul." He made no further argument.

Brendan lit a cigarette, and Colum watched as he held the flame in his big hands. How much he had changed. He was comparable to no one anymore. Brendan Donnelly was only like Brendan Donnelly. The few months had made such a difference. Colum wondered how he had come by it. Was it a result of the long tedious work at the Barrel Yard? The association with the older men who worked beside him until their deaths? The adulation of the women who had come to depend on him, whose lives were gathered about his habits and whimsies? The nervousness was gone and with it some of the earlier rambunctious charm and its attendant appeal for audience. He moved now in ordinary things—the choice of a doctor, the command for sanity, the placing of his hand on another man's shoulder, the ready whip of the tongue on one of his own—and he was easily the master of all that they entailed.

They heard a light knock on the door. Ellen answered it and said, "It's Father Moloney."

"Tell him come in," Brendan said.

The young priest entered the room. "Hello, again," he said.

"Hello, Father. Any news?" Brendan's voice wavered.

"Yes, there is. And for right now, we might consider it very good. As you know, the appendix ruptured." He seemed to say this for Colum's benefit. "They've operated and cut out the infected tissue. From this point on, she'll be given large injections of antibiotics—penicillin and the like. This is to ward off infection, to avoid the danger of peritonitis. Now it only remains to be seen what happens. She's resting. That's a good sign, they tell me. We must only trust now in God's holy will."

"Thank you, Father, for all you've done," Brendan said. "It was so late and all getting you out of bed."

"Isn't that my job, Brendie? Where would I be if it were all cake and ice cream?"

"How can we repay you, Father?" the mother asked.

"Don't even mention it. But what we can do before we go is get down on our knees and say a decade of the rosary for Josephine. Will you do that?"

"Yes," they all answered.

Colum found that the hard lino of the floor bruised his

shins. It had been months since he'd been on his knees. His hands hung awkwardly before him. He desperately sought to put them somewhere, attach them to something. Ellen noticed. She reached in her coat and handed him a rosary beads. He slowly wrapped it about his fist.

"The first Glorious Mystery, the Resurrection of Our Lord Jesus Christ from the dead. Our Father, Who art in Heaven, hallowed be Thy Name. Thy Kingdom come, Thy will be done on earth as it is in Heaven . . ."

Colum found his mouth enunciating the old words, not because he was suddenly gifted with a surge of faith, but only because they were harmless and not meant to bring pain or draw anger or deceive. And he had to admit that they had attached to them memories of happier days, praying by the fire as children, decades said in thanksgiving to St. Jude or the Virgin for favors received or for miraculous help needed on examinations. He felt the rough round texture of the beads as he clutched each one in its turn, feeling its full limit, and then moving with trepidation to the next. He was not unhappy. Nothing could touch him inside these words and inside this circle. He felt safe as he looked across at his brother whose eyes were closed in sincere prayer.

Chapter 59

Dawn on Sunday morning saw Colum and Brendan back again in the waiting room of Barrington's Hospital. Neither of them had slept very much, and the lack of food and warm drink was poor guard against the early cold of the hospital room. They walked back and forth in silence, strapping their hands about them. "What a country," Brendan said at last. "Warm cattle stalls, and freezing fucking hospitals."

"Shows you who comes first."

"Maybe we ought to have a bit of a fist fight to keep our blood thin."

They both laughed together.

The Donnelly name was called over the intercom. They banged into each other as they rushed for the door. They reached the front desk. The matron turned and asked, "Mr. Donnelly?"

"Both of us," Colum said.

"Oh," she answered and smiled. "Your sister is out of danger. You won't be able to see her for a while—tonight at the earliest—but no harm will come to her now. She had a good night."

They nodded.

"She'll need a lot of care. The weakness could come back on her. She's had a fearful bout."

"She'll get a lot of care," Brendan said.

On their way home, they stopped off at Angela Conway's pub in Sandmall. There was no hurry. By now, Ellen Sullivan would have driven their mother to the hospital as she had promised. The matron would give them the good news.

Angela was just opening for the day and cried out when she saw them, "Just what I need. Two strong men to lift down the shutters and break open a barrel. I'll treat you to your first one of the day."

Brendan unhooked the shutters, and Colum laid them carefully at the back of the snug, no longer used by the women and children as a sort of purgatory to the main bar. Together they hoisted the irons. These, too, were stored in the tight space.

The barrel itself was the easiest to secure, though the black stout shot past the worn pump washer, at one point, and soaked Colum's face. He could only laugh.

"Serves you right for being so greedy," Angela said and slapped him on the back. "Your father would have been proud of you. He was a great man for his early pint, God love him."

When the chores were completed, they sat down by the open fire, two whiskies and two pints before them. Above the grate, two chalk hurlers, painted to represent the colors of Limerick and those of Tipperary, did mock battle on their plaster field.

Angela called from the back of the pub. "Keep an eye on the counter for me, lads," she said. "I'm going out to the kitchen to put on a bit of pig's head for the dinner. If anyone comes in, just give them whatever they want. I'll add it up when I get back."

Colum sipped his strong drink. "I'm under a compliment to you," he said.

"For what?"

"For not mentioning what you found out."

"That you never worked for the *Herald?*"

"That I was chief editor for *Cumas.*"

"I didn't know *that.*"

"But you guessed?"

"I guessed that you were in there somewhere."

"What was it that gave you the clue?"

"The mention of the china dogs."

"Ha! Home and hearth gave me away. I never thought of that."

"We seldom give the small things much credit."

Brendan was silent for more than a minute. Then he said, "I have to hand it to you. That plan was nothing less than brilliant. Whose idea was it? McDavitt's? Riordan's?"

"Mine."

"Go on!"

"Yes."

"But tell me, how did you get into all of this? I seem to remember you telling me that you were no kind of patriot. You thought that patriotism was a cod."

"Patriotism is not necessary at the middle. You won't find

a one at *Cumas*. It's just for the poor fools who are sucked in by the flags and songs and slogans. All made up, I might add, by men who haven't the foggiest notion of country or homeland."

"Their aim being?"

"Self. The game. Having people dance to your tune. Moving them like puppets. Antagonizing . . ."

"Putting the fuck to decent misfortunes."

"Sometimes causing their deaths." His head was bowed and his eyes were closed.

"Jesus Christ in heaven! What came over you, Colum? You were never made like that."

"I'll tell you."

And Colum was as good as his word. He spilled out the details like some scrupulous penitent, pausing now and then to explain more thoroughly the implications of each facet, each motivation, each hue and color of his involvement. He spared himself nothing. Not once did he raise his head or look to see the reaction in the other's face for fear that the telling might become its own end and the taint might linger with him to fester again at a later time. He wanted it all out, all out into the smoky air of the little pub.

Brendan spoke. "We've got to think about getting you out. If that's what you want."

"All I know is that I don't want to go back."

"But it's not like an ordinary job. You should know that. You just don't say, 'I quit.' "

"But you got out."

"They were fed up with me. And I didn't know as much as you do. You've seen them at their heart. If you leave all of a sudden, they'll think that it's your intention to inform."

"But you saw Riordan's face . . ."

"They had my patriotism to count on. They knew that I'd never turn them in."

"But why would I . . ."

"Well, Colum," Brendan said, "I don't know how to put

this. But you were bought once—by them. What's to keep them from thinking that you cannot be bought again? If they know themselves, they know you."

Colum did not speak for the longest time. Then he said, "You're right. But what must I do?"

"Go back."

"Back?"

"Yes. Go through the motions for a bit. Certain things are afoot. I don't think that they'll be riding so high after a short while."

"The elections?"

"I'll tell you when you get back next weekend. But one thing I want you to do. Will you pass on a word for me?"

"Certainly."

"Here it is. The next time you see Riordan, simply say, 'I guess my brother, Brendan, did it all on his own.' 'All on his own?' he'll ask. You say, 'Yes.' 'What are you talking about?' he'll say. Then, very casually, answer, 'Well, he's just a step away from pinpointing Liam Daly's killer.' Oh, that'll get him."

"Have you really come close to finding out who did it?"

"Yes. It was done from the inside."

"Oh, my God." He shivered.

"But you'll do that?"

"Sure. Why not?"

"Thanks. I just want to show him."

They drank their glasses of porter, and Brendan went to the bar for refills. It would be a long day until it was time again to go back to the hospital.

Chapter 60

J osie's face looked drawn as she rested against the pillows of the bed. Colum stooped to kiss her.

"Oh, my Lord," she said. "We'll be arrested."

He brushed her pale skin with his lips. "I'll be back on the weekend," he said.

"You promise?"

"I'll put my life on it."

"Good. We'll have ham and turkey and trifle . . ."

The mother interrupted. "We'll have no such thing. You're going to be in your bed for two or three weeks. If he comes up, he'll be doing it for the sake of seeing our ugly faces—not to fill his belly."

"I wasn't talking about me," Josie said. "Brendan can cook as good as anyone. He's going out this week with a list of the things I had planned. Aren't you, Brendan?"

Brendan smiled. "Jesus!" he said. "They get one bit sick and they become bloody tyrants."

His mother, at first, turned the side of her face to Colum when he kneeled to kiss her. But suddenly, reconsidering her action, she clutched him tightly about the neck, her fingers tearing into his flesh. "Godspeed," she whispered. "We'll be waiting for you on Friday."

Brendan shook his hand. "Good luck," he said, "and remember what I told you to do."

"With Riordan?"

"Yes."

"I'll do it the first thing that I see him."

"Right."

He met Ellen on the hospital steps. She was on her way in. "You're going already?" she said.

"Yes. But I'll be back for the holidays."

"Will you be here over the New Year?"

"I might be able to manage that. Why?"

She looked away. "Oh, nothing," she said.

"What? Tell me."

"It's just that the college is having a bit of a dance. I was wondering if you'd be interested in . . ."

"I'd like that. We can count on it, then."

"Colum, if you don't want . . ."

"I do."

She touched his arm. "Drive safely," she said.

"I will."

Colum counted and dreaded each successive step as he descended into the depths of the *Cumas* building. He came to the final door. He placed a nervous hand on the brass knob and turned. The lock slid back easily. Now he stood in the full light of the underground center.

His fear left him for a moment. The atmosphere of the place was like that of any Monday morning. The phone lights flashed. The steam rose from the hot cups of tea. The bright lights created no shadows. Cleary and Mangan were already at their desks.

At the sight of him, the two men rose and walked in his direction. Mangan was the first to speak. "Colum," he said, "we heard. We're awfully sorry."

"Are you all right yourself?" Cleary asked.

"Yes." So they knew only that Sean had been shot and that he had escaped. Nothing more. For a moment he felt their adulation. He was a hero to them by the mere fact that he had survived, pushed his way out, and was now back at his desk to continue again his valuable work. How many times he himself had made heroes out of mere blackguards in a similar manner. Even now he felt the old weakness haunt him. "Listen," he said, "I've got to get on the story. I'll fill you in on all the details later."

And he knew that they must have thought him a thorough professional as he walked to his office and began leafing through his papers. No matter how he turned, they were ready to see him as their superior; there was no getting away from it. He wanted to cry out to them, "Stop! Stop! For my sake and yours, stop!" But he remembered Brendan's words—"Go through the motions for a bit." And his brother had spoken of murder. God, it was hard to imagine the taint of that in connection with this clean lighted place or with any of its affairs. Even the memory of Dermot O'Murchu's face sneering up at him didn't seem quite enough. Certainly, the terrorist was suspected of murder, but that had never been proved beyond a shadow of a doubt. Maybe he should never have come back, he thought. He should have run with his natural terror and taken the consequences. This place was enchanted . . .

Riordan did not arrive until Tuesday. Colum looked up from his desk and saw the gaunt figure in the outer doorway. His heart beat against his ribs. He experienced the same suffocation of Saturday night. He saw the old man smile to the others and walk towards his office.

When Riordan had seated himself, he smiled. "You're all right, Colum," he said.

"Yes."

"That's what counts."

"But Sean Keane is dead, ready to be put in his grave . . ."

Riordan's face darkened. "I won't hear that," he said with severity. "There was nothing that could be done. You're lucky that you're not in a coffin yourself. Those bastards were so keyed up that they'd have shot their own mothers. You must not think of it as your error. I want you never to say to yourself that you killed him. That's an order."

The blood rushed to his head. He had no illusions. Here was the truth of what he had suspected. Pretending to glance at one of the papers on his desk, he said, "When did you hear yourself?"

"Not until we were safe in Cashel."

"I see."

Riordan lit a cigarette. "Were you able to get on the story?" he said.

"Not yet. I was home over the weekend."

"Home?" His eyes darted in his head.

"Yes. My sister was shifted to the hospital. Her appendix burst. She's all right now. But I'll have to go back there next weekend."

"Certainly. Take whatever time you need. We'll close down for Christmas, anyway. It wouldn't do to give the impression of not honoring the religious season."

"No."

Riordan seemed to sink deeper into the chair. "And your brother," he said, "how is he these days?"

Here it was. He looked straight into the old man's eyes. He felt somehow a surge of perverse pleasure when he said, "Fine. I guess he did it all on his own."

"All on his own?"

"Yes."

"What are you talking about?"

"Well, he says he's just a step away from pinpointing Liam Daly's killer."

Riordan's face became contorted. The cigarette dropped onto his lap. He violently brushed the red ashes from his coat. "Damn that brother of yours," he said. "Can't he leave very well alone? That little bastard and weakling did away with himself. Why does that other fool have to keep meddling? He'll be the death of all of us. He'll bring the roof down on top of us." He stood up and left the office without a further word.

Chapter 61

Brendan hoisted the last barrel onto the Guinness lorry. Jaggers pressed on the hooter to indicate that he was pulling away from the wooden ramp. It was three o'clock. All the next day's deliveries were loaded.

He heard Shanahan's voice call from the office. "Brendie," the foreman said. "Brendie."

"Yes."

"There's a man here to see you. Hurry up."

He wiped his face with his handkerchief and replaced the cloth in his sleeve. He walked towards the office. Probably one of the union stewards after him again. The man had been all plamas the last time. Perhaps this was the time for severity. Join. Join. That was all you heard these days. He'd had enough of bloody joining, he thought.

The figure that stood in the doorway was not unfamiliar to him. The lines beneath the eyes. The cruel mouth. The powerful droop of the shoulders. Garoid Sheridan. Riordan's top man in the city. He hadn't expected so sudden a response. Colum had made good use of his time.

"Brendan," Sheridan said and extended his hand.

Brendan took it. "Hello, Garoid," he said.

"We haven't seen much of you in the past months. Not even at a meeting."

"I've been busy here. The job is a ball crusher."

"Sure, I know what you mean. Well, Brendie, I was wondering if we might have a bit of a chat somewhere quiet. It wouldn't take long."

"Behind the shed."

They walked to the rear of the holding warehouse and sat on a low wall that bordered the yard.

Sheridan was the first to speak. "I've been talking to Taig," he said, "and he's awfully anxious to get you back into the swing of things. We don't find them with your expertise every day, you know."

"Thanks."

"What I'm asking is this: Would you be open to doing an occasional job for us? I mean . . ."

"I might be."

"The money would be good."

"I'd like that."

"First, of course, Taig would have to have a bit of a talk with you to explain fully. I'm not even in on the details myself. But I gather he has something special in mind for that eye and arm of yours."

"It's fine with me."

Sheridan fingered the top button of his gabardine. "When would I set up the meeting?" he said.

"Anytime."

"It would have to be out of the city."

"That's no bother."

"Well, he's off to Dublin tomorrow. God knows where he's spending Christmas. Would tonight be too sudden?"

"No. Not at all."

"Any particular place?"

"Where is he now?"

"Kilkenny."

"I could meet him at Bouladoff—it's halfway."

"The town?"

"There's a bit of a wood this side of the town. It's a stone's throw from the Suir river."

"I know it—Green Wood."

"The same."

"The time?"

"Eight o'clock."

"He'll be there, I promise you."

"Eight, then."

"Right."

"Tell him thanks for remembering me again."

"Tell him yourself—ha!"

"I forgot," he said and laughed.

Sheridan walked to the edge of the cobblestones. A

maroon Granada drove up to meet him. He got in.

A faint bitter smile crossed Brendan's face as he returned to his work.

Back in the hut, the men were having their afternoon tea break. As Brendan entered, Joe Hassett, the crane man, motioned him to sit down. "The Primate, Brendan," he said, "the Primate of all Ireland, Cardinal Gostrey. He's on the wireless, giving out of him . . ."

Brendan took his place and began to unscrew the cork of his flask. The country voice boomed above him:

> Inevitably, in a situation of emergency, a
> government has to take certain actions which lessen
> human liberty. At any given time, it is difficult
> to assess whether they have gone too far or not in that
> process. I wouldn't feel that the government has
> gone too far. I would feel, though, that some of the
> measures—like the Criminal Law (Jurisdiction)
> Bill—ought not to be kept in force one day longer than is
> necessary . . .

> . . . This is a complex thing, but, statistically,
> something is happening now. If you take the macro
> situation, the violence is less, measured by
> statistics. What is happening is that, among the tiny
> minorities of violent men, there is a certain
> fragmentation going on. And the tiny fragmented groups
> are in one sense being more horrific in what
> they're doing . . .

> . . . Nonsense! Nonsense! All evidence goes to
> show that not only would integrated education not help
> the Catholic-Protestant situation, it would harm
> it. Not only would it not strengthen a pluralist society, it
> is directly contrary to the principles of
> pluralism. . . . That some politicians should feel that it is
> necessary to kill the Catholic devotional life in
> the schools in order to have good relations between

Catholics and Protestants in the Republic is the
height of absurdity. A pluralist society is a rope of
many-colored threads: you don't put it into a
washbasin and blend all the colors together . . .

Great God, Brendan thought. Words upon words upon
words. Like the drink—the Irish comfort and disease. Even in
the elect!

Chapter 62

Riordan did not leave his office once during the day. But
Colum watched the special telephone indicator light
up five or six times. He began to wonder if his words
about Daly's killer had not begun something sinister.

He waited until the last minute. Mangan and Cleary had
left for the day. He looked down at the row of buttons on his
telephone. Riordan's indicator was on again. What if he
lifted the receiver and listened in? he thought. He decided
against that. He realized that this was not child's play.

The lights went off. He heard shuffling noises in the next
room. The door opened. He heard a loud crash as Riordan
slammed it behind him. This was followed by a faint but
distinct double click of the lock. Colum held his breath. The
bolt had not engaged. Would the old man notice it? He
counted to ten. Thank God he hadn't!

Colum waited for almost twenty minutes before making
his move. What if Riordan forgot something? Or was merely
running to his car? Or down the street for cigarettes? He
couldn't risk discovery. He looked at his watch. He'd given
him enough time. He walked slowly towards the curtained
office. His hand reached out and pushed the knob. The door
opened before him.

What was he looking for? he asked himself. He didn't know exactly. If anything, the object of his search would be in or on the desk—the rest of the room was bare and without shelves or furniture of any kind. He eased back the swivel chair and sat down. He switched on the desk lamp.

So this was the seat of power, the center of all the strings to all the cat's-paws? And this was the hollow room that he had so often wished to be made welcome in? The thoughts depressed him. He put them from his mind and began with apprehension to search through the carelessly piled folders in the desk. (It looked as though they had been randomly gathered and dumped into the drawer.) But he found little of interest. Clippings from newspapers. Maps of cities and villages. Photographs of Garda barracks.

When he replaced the files, he noticed that the base of the drawer was loose and made a slight rattling sound. He lifted the papers back onto the desk, and examined the steel plating beneath. It was notched on one side. He placed his index finger in the crimps and lifted. The steel cover to the lower compartment raised easily. The cavity contained two manila folders.

He placed the first before him in the light. Across its face was marked a large red X. The name at the top startled him. It read:

LIAM FINTAN DALY

He nervously raised the cover and looked at the sheet within. Slowly he followed the report of the boy's activities over the few months of his membership in the organization. The last paragraph stood out like an epitaph. It was written in Riordan's hand:

Word received that Daly followed Donnelly
from Adare to Laffey's pub. Was observed watching
from doorway. Identity later confirmed by me.

Must have seen my face clearly. Knows too much for his
own good.

Colum dropped the folder onto the desk. He lifted the
second file. A similar X was scratched across the yellow
cardboard. The name at the top was all too familiar to him:

BRENDAN MICHAEL DONNELLY

He opened the folder. It contained the reports of Brendan's
various assignments over the last year. It ended with the
ambush at Annacotty.

He began to search frantically for something else, some
date, some indication of a plot against his own flesh and
blood. But what? Where? He examined the blotter on the
desk. It was spotless, not so much as the scratch of a pen. He
went back through the top folders again. Nothing.

Then it came to him. Why hadn't he thought of it before?
With the door presumed to be locked, Riordan would have
no reason for excessive secrecy. (No great cunning had been
involved in the placement of the folders in the lower
compartment of the desk.) He reached under the steel frame
and pulled out the wastebasket. He looked in. It contained a
crumpled Gold Flake package and a tiny wad of notepaper.
He opened the paper. Across it were scribbled the words:

GREEN WOOD—BOULADOFF—8 O'CLOCK

He paused. So this had been Brendan's dead serious game,
and he had fallen prey to it. Brendan Donnelly, who saw
himself as the last good man, riding out like some heroic
chieftain to protect the lives of his own and those that
depended upon him, because he saw that his notion of honor
was manacled and that he was the one remaining arbiter of
relentless justice. And what about himself, Colum Donnelly?
Would his role be that of disinterested observer and would

he later rationalize the death of his own kind? Wouldn't this objective stand be the fine and finished product of all that *Cumas* had preached and he had taken to so readily—no feeling for the outer world, and now no feeling for those of his very family? He thought of his father's medieval philosophy of life. Family was all. From there the limits spiraled in or out. Self was all. Or every man, woman, and child counted. He felt ashamed, now, that he had taken the inward road, and Brendan, for all his romanticism and wildness, had moved into the future. He had cared for his own flesh and was about to take upon himself the responsibility of revenge for a stranger's murder. He looked out desperately at Sean Keane's empty desk. Suddenly, he saw clearly before him his friend's face, the face filled with terror that he had deserted in the train station just a few days before. He remembered, too, the faces of the men and women he had encountered on the streets and in the laneways of Kildare as he had pushed roughly against them in his flight from the Guards. Faces filled with a similar alarm. Ordinary men and women in dread of their very lives. Sheep being led to the slaughter. And he had been the movement's drover, of a kind, a prodder and a jabber, a gamester, a bully, an inquisitor of the worst order. Could it be said of him, he asked himself, that he was, from a calculated point in his life, a dead thing without love nor comfort?

He did not stop to grab his overcoat but was out into the gathering twilight like a shot.

Chapter 63

The man at the sports store smiled as he wrapped the Webley pistol in a cardboard box and placed a carton of .38 caliber shells beside it. "Are you going to shoot yourself a Guard," he said and laughed. "Or are you out to get yourself a boyo?"

Colum adjusted the glasses on his face. "No," he said. "It's for my Mam in Waterford. Her flat has been broken into four times in the last year and a half."

"Jesus! Isn't it a terrible disgrace? And the Guards are helpless to do a thing about it. Hitler should have won the war. It's a deal of jackeens that'd be running around on the streets, then, I can tell you that."

"You might be right."

"Will she be afraid of it?"

"What?"

"The Webley. It has a kick, you know."

"I'll give her a lesson or two. I was in the Army for about a year when I first got out of school," he lied.

"Oh, you'll have no bother then. You probably knew the ins and outs of it a long time ago."

"It's been a few years. It's a good thing you went over it with me. Things change."

"You think that the Webley's changed! You should see the others. You could write ten books on the modifications."

"I'd say."

Colum filled out the ownership form, placing a false name and address on it. He had reached for his license earlier, but the clerk had waved it away, saying that the formalities were more of a nuisance than anything. "What good is a license or a dispensary card?" he'd said. "You can buy them on any corner. I never bother to ask—no one knows who's who in this country anymore. People don't know their own names, for Christ's sake. What you put on here is your own business. If you kill someone, I'll swear that you had identification cards coming out your arsehole."

As Colum walked towards the door, the clerk called after him. "Hey," he said.

He froze as he turned to face the red-faced man.

"Tell your mother to shoot all of them blackguards, if she can. Fill them full of holes like a sieve."

"I will."

He hurried into the Christmas crowds in Pennyfeather Lane.

Chapter 64

The drive to Bouladoff was tiring, especially after the long day's work. Brendan had to open the side vents of the Morris Minor on several occasions along the way and allow the cold air to shock his face. Perhaps he should have set a later night in the week, suggested a nearer rendezvous . . . He had waited long enough. He had even suspected that he might not go through with it. But the chain had begun.

Green Wood was situated to the west of Bouladoff. At one time, it had been used for Army gymkhanas and a clearing had been cut at its center. He knew it well. His company had camped on the open ground for several nights a few years back. He remembered the bashes, the fights, and the town girls who had sneaked past the sentries and into the compound of oilcloth tents. And the fifteen men who had caught the pox as a result. He laughed to himself as he left the road. He had bypassed the usual entrance to the wood and driven further north along the country boreen that bordered the ring of dark trees. He counted on Riordan not being familiar with the lay of the land. That was his only advantage, and he knew it.

He parked the car near a large cement culvert and started across the field towards the nearest cluster of trees. He would try, however, to keep his distance from them so as to avoid having the brambles crack beneath his feet. He would find the narrow riverbed that angled south and through the heart of the break. The sand and gravel would muffle the sound of his footsteps.

In the moonlight, he could see the passage between the trees. He took every step carefully like some First Communion child on her way to the altar. Bit by tiny bit, the space narrowed. If he could get inside the compound, he could then lie in the deep grass and listen for giveaway sounds. He was sure that they would come from the south of him. Riordan had no reason to suspect that he knew yet of his guilt. The old man would be more inclined to walk right up to him and empty his gun. The thought sent the fire through him as he remembered how Liam had been butchered.

He was nearing his spot at last. Not more than twenty yards to go. The precision of his steps tired him. His feet ached and the muscles in his legs were knotted in pain. Perhaps when he reached the grassy bank he could rest. It was not yet eight o'clock. There were at least ten minutes left. He had noticed no sign of cars on the road. He was the first here, surely.

Suddenly, he lost his footing. He fell backwards, his feet making a great splash in the near frozen pool beneath him. He clutched the Luger firmly and tried to brace himself with his left hand.

The first thing he saw was the flash of the gun not fifteen yards from him. Almost in the same instant, he felt the shell pass within an inch of his face. He flattened out in the cold icy water. He slowly raised the Luger and waited. He had to get his bearings on the other's exact location. He counted the seconds. One. Two. Three. Nothing. Not even a sound. He reached across and picked up a heavy stone. He threw it into the deeper area of the pool. It sent shards of water flying into the moonlight.

Immediately, the gun spat its blue fire. Brendan had the spot now. He squeezed the trigger firmly. One shot. A pause. Then another. He heard a violent scream, and a heavy crash followed it.

He waited for almost five minutes before crawling out of his pit and up the embankment. He felt his way through the coarse and prickly grass. His clothes were freezing against him.

He saw it ahead of him—the outline of a man lying face up

in the thicket. He crept closer. He saw the face in the clear light. It was that of McDavitt. And there was not a stir out of him.

He crouched to his knees. The Luger was still in his hand. He felt real terror for the first time in his life. He had often boasted of how it would be no bother to him. Now it was a reality. He had killed a human being.

Seconds passed before he realized his danger. Where was Rior . . .

The voice was mocking. It came from behind him. "Drop the gun," he said. "Drop it."

Chapter 65

Colum looked at his watch as he parked the Volkswagen in the gravel lot to the south of Green Wood. Seven minutes to eight. He cursed the heavy traffic on the road. But it looked as though no one were here. No cars. No sounds. Just a deserted wood in the middle of the beyond. What if he'd been wrong, if it had been all a balk?

Just then, he heard the crack of a gun somewhere north of him and towards the center of the wood. He dropped to his knees and loaded the Webley. He prayed that he'd gotten the clerk's directions right.

Again, he heard a shot. It was followed by two more. Then came a scream that sent chills through him. What if it were . . .

He found a gully that ran north through the ring of trees. He lowered his head and began to run along its boundary. Sharp blackthorn bushes tore at his face. The thick grass snared his feet, and he fell headlong on two occasions. He knew that his right hand was bleeding, though he was aware of no pain, only the wetness of the shirt against his flesh.

At first, he mistook the low sound in the distance for that of a brook. But as he gained yards, he was aware of voices. He moved, ever so slowly, in their direction.

He could hear them now though he could not distinguish the exact words. Just a few more feet, he told himself. He slid along on his belly over the stones and frozen mud. He guessed that the conversation was taking place not thirty yards from where he lay.

At last the voices became clear. In the night air, Riordan's usual pitch was distorted and seemed foreign to him. But its message was clear.

"You stupid peasant," Riordan was saying. "You and the rest of the imbeciles that make up this ignorant . . ."

Colum stood up. Before him in the moonlight he saw the tall silhouette of Riordan. To the right, on his knees, was Brendan, bowed like some supplicant before a dark idol. How dare this monster humiliate and shame one of his own!

His hands trembling, he raised the Webley. He fired once. He fired again. He fired a third time. At last, the shadow dropped and became part of the blackness below it. Only Brendan's profile stood out against the moon.

Chapter 66

A half hour had passed, and they made their way towards the boreen. "What will we do from here?" Colum said.

"We'll go on because there's nothing else that we can do. We'll go on and take the good with the bad."

"But Riordan and his . . ."

"We'll pay for that in our own way. We're all guilty, you

know. You, me, the next man. And there'll be the devil to suffer. We stood by and let it happen—to ourselves and to the country of ours. We knew bloody well what was going on all the time. Oh, God, did we know! We had no blinders on at all!"

"You're right."

They reached the gravel road. In a matter of twenty minutes, they had left Green Wood, and the pitch of the night seemed to draw them like tiny fireflies into itself.